Two Hours Til Open

TARA MONTGOMERY

TARA MONTGOMERY

Copyright © 2024 Tara Montgomery
All rights reserved.
ISBN: 9798327817517

TARA MONTGOMERY

DEDICATION

This book is dedicated to all the women who have had to make hard decisions to keep your mind and soul. You are not alone.

"Things in the game done changed, real talk!"

Dave Hollister

ACKNOWLEDGMENTS

I want to acknowledge all the family and friends that were a part of the creation of this project. I especially acknowledge the men in my life that answered my silly questions in the quest to create authentic characters. Thank you all.
Mommy, I did it!

1 THE BEGINNING OF THE END

Kimberly opened the basement door and stared down the stairs. This area of her home has always been used as her husband's man cave, but after today, she was sure that she would see it as something different. She took a deep breath as she thought to walk away and forget the whole thing. There was nothing that said she had to go through with it. It wasn't like she had signed some kind of contract. She could change her mind. It was her right, right?

Of course, it was, but she knew that she would not change her mind. This was her own idea. How could she change her mind on something that she had suggested? If Kimberly changed her mind, it would make her look indecisive and unsure of herself. Not to mention, it would put them right back where they started, and her sole intent was to change the nature of their relationship. No, she would not change her mind. Not only would she go through with it, but she would do it so well that, her husband would have no idea that she didn't want to do it.

What she wanted was for him to love her unconditionally. Kimberly wanted her husband to want no other woman. She wanted him to cringe at the thought of another man touching her and to see her as the center of his universe. Instead, she has caught him in many compromising situations of extramarital affairs. As a result, of his cheating, Kimberly has had a few extracurricular activities of her own. She participated in these indiscretions as a retaliation. She needed him to understand the feeling of betrayal and mistrust. She wanted him to learn that it was not normal for a couple to be bonded and commit such treachery against one another.

Carl never caught Kimberly in any of these affairs. She confessed of her own freewill. She tried to keep it a secret in hopes that he would be able to figure it out, but he never said a word. He went about his daily life without interruption, oblivious to what she felt, was staring him in the face. Kimberly didn't know if he was just ignoring the signs, or if he just didn't care.

Later, she learned that he did care. When Kimberly confessed, he remained quiet and seemingly, unmoved. He walked away from her and stood in front of the wall on the far side of the room. After a few minutes, he punched his fist through the wall, turned and glared at her over his shoulder. Next, he left and did not return that day.

When he finally showed up at the house two days later, he was very angry. He told Kimberly that he would never be able to forgive her. He said that he would never see her the same. He no longer trusted her and was unsure if he wanted to remain in the marriage.

It was this event that led them to marriage counseling. They saw two different counselors over a two-year period. The first of which Carl said he didn't like or trust. The second was a female that seemed more interested in hanging on to Carl's every word, than in trying to help save the couple's marriage.

After all was said and done, the couple wanted to go their separate ways, but their financial situation made it impossible. It seemed that neither could survive without the help of the other. They also shared a large amount of joint debts. For this reason, they decided that it would be more beneficial to stay together.

As a result, the couple decided that they would try to push through their many problems. Kimberly suggested that they create their own definition of marriage and classify their relationship according to what worked best for the two of them, as a unit. She decided that they would or should no longer let the traditional societal views of marriage distinguish who and what they would be. This was when she brought up the idea of starting an open relationship.

Carl's first reaction to her suggestion was one of disbelief. He laughed, like she had just told the funniest joke that he had ever heard in his life. When she told him that she was serious, he became skeptical.

Kimberly's logic was that since the two of them could not be faithful to one another, then maybe they shouldn't be. If both agreed that it was okay to have other sexual partners, it would take the strain off of trying to remain faithful and the barriers of trust would be taken down. She rationalized that he would no longer have to worry about her questioning his whereabouts and she would not have to deal with the idea of him messing around behind her back.

As Carl began to consider her proposition, he realized that there could be some benefits, as well as losses. He would be free to roam as he pleased, but he would also have to live with the idea that Kimberly would be free to do the same. He would no longer have to hide telephone numbers in his cell phone or disguise the women on his Facebook, Instagram, and Twitter pages. At the same time, he would have to live with these situations for his wife as well.

To Kimberly's surprise, Carl's response to

her idea was negative. He declined the idea of opening their marriage and held firm to the idea of monogamy. His explanation was that he was having a hard enough time moving past the image of her with someone else. He could not be intimate with a woman that has had sexual relations with numerous men. There was a part of her that was delighted that he would be so jealous, because it was never her intention to sleep with any other men. She had only suggested the idea as an attempt to give herself a sense of peace while keeping her marriage at the same time. So, with his rejection, Kimberly let go of the idea.

    Today, it had been over a year since that initial conversation. Two weeks ago, Karl reintroduced the idea. He said that he had not cheated on her, but he was admitting that it was getting harder for him to remain faithful. He said that he could no longer do it behind her back, especially since she had given him the option not to. When Kimberly asked about how he felt about her with other men, he stated that it would be something he would just have to learn to live with. So, they agreed to give the idea of an open relationship a try and decided that before anyone did anything, they would settle on some rules that both would have to abide by. They decided that they would think about what they wanted individually and would come back in two weeks to discuss it. While they were thinking about it, Karl suggested that, as a commemoration of the start of the new relationship, both would have sex with someone else at the same time, so no one would feel guilty about being the first. Kimberly agreed and today was the day that they would discuss the rules. It was also the day that they would both have sex with someone else.

The couple decided that they would individually invite another person into their home, the intent here, to remain private and somewhat together at the same time. They would do it in two separate rooms of the house and come out and discuss the events with one another afterwards. But, before any of this could happen, they needed to come together to discuss the rules.

This is what was about to happen as Kimberly stood at the top of the basement stairs. Carl had been down here all morning. This was his man cave and he spent most of his time in the home in this location. He had a pool table and all his game systems down in the basement. There was also a wet bar, spare bedroom, and full bathroom. He had couches and a computer set up in the large space as well. The basement was the equivalent of a small apartment or what a single man would call a bachelor pad.

Kimberly walked down the stairs. As she neared the bottom, she could see Carl sitting on the couch. He was laid back with his head on one of the smaller pillows. He seemed to be engrossed in whatever program was playing on the television. The stairs ended a few feet behind the back of the couch, so Kimberly could not see his face. She walked around the side of the couch and sat down beside him. Her gaze locked on the television. She felt afraid to look at him. She did not know what his facial expression would be. She feared that he might have a look of excitement, while hers was one of hesitation. Carl did not move or look in her direction. After a few moments of silence, she slowly turned her gaze toward him. Her eyes remained low and trained on his legs. She slowly raised them up his body, noticing that his breathing seemed calm and relaxed. His legs were extended, indicating that there was no tension in his body. She continued her screen up toward his chest and to his neck. Next, she looked at his chin, then his nose, and reluctantly into his eyes. She noticed that his eyes were already on her. A bit startled, Kimberly dropped her gaze for a moment. She then lifted her eyes again to look at his face but said nothing. She noticed a small smile form on his face as he took her hand. Kimberly felt a sense of calm come over her. Maybe, he was going to tell her that he changed his mind again and that he couldn't go through with it. Maybe he realized how important their relationship was to him and was going to tell her how much he cherished her. He opened his mouth to speak. Kimberly held her breath. Tears formed in her eyes and then he said the words that would signify the beginning of the end.

"Are you ready?"

TWO HOURS TIL OPEN

PART ONE

TARA MONTGOMERY

2 THE RULES OF THE GAME

"Are you ready?"

"I just asked you."

"I believe I am," Kimberly said. "Have you thought about your rules?"

"Yeah, I thought about a few things but nothing extravagant. How about you?"

"I thought about a few things, but I don't think I'll really be able to decide until we actually start doing things. I mean, I don't know what to consider."

"Well, you can't be changing the rules once it gets started, Kim."

"I don't mean changing them, just altering things that don't work. We should know when it happens, Carl."

"I hear you, but you can't just be altering the rules just to fit your personal comfort."

"It won't be anything like that, Carl. I just don't want us to forget anything important."

"Well, we won't know what's important until we actually start doing things."

Kimberly sat in silence as she continued to

look into his face. She wanted to tell him that she really didn't want to go through with this. That she had changed her mind, but she was afraid. She did not want to lose her husband. At this point, she was willing to do whatever it took to save her marriage and family. She did not want to see her children grow up in a home without their father.

"Just promise me that we will always be here for one another, no matter what. Promise me that this won't come between us."

"If it starts coming between us, we'll stop it instantly. Is that fair?" Carl asked.

"I guess so," Kimberly answered.

"So, what else you got? What are your rules?"

"Well, I have been thinking about this and making sure I understand what it means to have an open relationship. My definition is that we both get to have sex with other people of our choice. Is that how you define it too?" She asked.

"Pretty much."

"Okay, and we are only talking about sex, right? Just the physical act?"

"Sure."

"Don't say sure, Carl. Answer the question."

"I did. Yes, just sex," he hissed.

"Okay, then that means there can be no emotional involvement with anyone."

"All right, I can live with that."

"Good, so that means that you can't sleep with the same person more than once. Repeat occasions tend to lead to emotional involvement."

"I don't know if I like that idea," Carl said.

"Why not?"

"Because sometimes I might enjoy myself enough to want to try it again with someone. That doesn't mean that I'm going to fall in love with them."

"They might fall in love with you. You know a woman's emotions seem to be tied to her vagina for some reason."

"That's not my problem if she falls in love."

"Yes, it is, Carl. You need to do whatever it takes to avoid that. That's why we need to stick with one encounter per person."

"Okay, how about no more than two."

"All right," Kimberly said reluctantly. "I'll compromise on two, but if you feel yourself getting emotionally involved, you have to be honest and tell me."

"That goes for you too, right?"

"Absolutely."

"So, what else?" He asked.

"It's your turn," Kimberly responded.

"Um, let me think."

"I thought you said you already thought about it. What are you still trying to figure out."

"I'm making sure I say the right thing."

"Don't just say the right thing. Say what's on your mind, Carl."

"All right. No exes."

"What?"

"You can't get with anyone that you've already been with."

"You mean we right? We can't get with anyone that we've been with in the past."

"Yes, I meant both of us. Not just you."

"Okay, I can live with that. Also, we have to tell the other before we do anything."

"I don't like that one. Sometimes things just happen. It's not always planned."

"Carl, you are the first person to say that a woman knows first if she's going to sleep with a man or not. Things don't just happen."

"You're right but just because she knows doesn't mean that I do."

"Okay fine, but we must tell each other about every encounter, before or after. We don't go to sleep without telling the other," Kimberly said.

"I can live with that."

"Also, when we get with one another. You have to tell if you have just been with someone else. We owe that courtesy to one another."

"That's fair."

"No staying out overnight," Kimberly said. "And none of these excursions can interfere with any family plans."

"What do you mean interfere?" Carl asked.

"I mean, if we have something planned, you cannot change to go get with some woman. The family still comes first."

"I got it. What else?"

"It's your turn."

"You can't be questioning the women I get with, and you can't get mad. No judging."

"All right, but the same goes for you."

"Deal." Carl said. "Anything else?"

"Oh yes, never in our bed."

"Definitely. Or in our house, after today."

"Okay, that's only right."

"Absolutely."

"Well, I can't think of anything else right now. I think I'm done. Oh wait, my friends are off-limits."

"Oh, come on. You don't think I would stoop that low, do you?" Carl laughed.

"I don't know, Carl. You never cease to amaze me sometimes."

"Aw, that's messed up. Come on now. I'm better than that. Plus, all your friends talk too much anyway."

"Shut up. No, they don't," Kimberly laughed. "Speaking of talking too much. No one can know that we are doing this. Not even the person you're with."

"Sometimes they need to know to ease the

situation."

"No, Carl. No one can know. If you can't agree to this, the deal is off."

"I don't see what the big deal is. No one cares what we do in our marriage."

"Are you crazy? Everyone cares, especially nosy people."

"Okay fine, no one will know."

"Thank you. I mean, I can't believe I'm doing this to begin with. The last thing I need is the world knowing that I have allowed such craziness into my home."

"Why are you ashamed?"

"I don't know if ashamed is the word."

"Then what's the word?" Carl asked.

"I'm not sure what the word is right now, but I'll let you know as soon as I figure it out."

"I think you already know."

"I don't. I just don't know if this is the healthiest thing to be doing for our relationship or for my self-esteem."

"And what the hell does that mean, Kimberly?"

"It just means that this is a huge sacrifice to be making just to save a marriage, that's all I'm saying?"

"Sacrifice?"

"Yes, how many women do you know that will let their man have sex with other women and want to know about it?"

"I don't care what other women or other people think. It's all about what we think. I mean you were the one that said we shouldn't let the traditional rules and people's narrow-minded perceptions define our marriage."

"I never said anything about people's narrow-minded perceptions."

"You did say traditional rules."

"Yes, I did, but…, never mind. You're right," Kimberly said quietly."

"But what, Kimberly? What were you about to say?"

"Nothing, Carl. I wasn't going to say anything?"

"Yes, you were, Kim. Say it."

"I was going to say that I said that when I was worried about losing you. I thought that you were on the verge of leaving me and the kids. I wanted you to know how much I loved you and to let you know that there was nothing that I wasn't willing to do to keep you. I don't know; now that I look back on it, it doesn't look good for my self-worth. I feel like I put you ahead of my esteem," she said."

"What? What do you mean? You don't think I'm good enough to fight for? Is that what you're saying, Kim?"

"No Carl, that's not what I'm saying. You have to be able to see that this isn't about you. I just feel like if I was thinking properly, I would not have presented this to you. I was just so fed up with you cheating on me; I was trying to say and do anything that would change your behavior. I wasn't thinking about how any of my decisions would affect any other areas of my life."

"So, you are saying that you really don't want to do this? You're only doing it for me?"

"That's not what I'm saying," Kimberly answered, saying the exact opposite of what she was really thinking.

"Sounds like you are," Carl said. "Look, let's just forget the whole thing. We can call them and tell them not to come. I mean, they are going to be here in less than two hours but it's not too late to stop them."

"I don't want to stop them, Carl. I'm just telling you how I felt at the time when this all started."

"Really. So how do you feel right now, Kim?"

"Afraid, Carl. Like I don't know what I'm doing."

"Then why are you doing it?"

"Because I said I would and part of me is curious as to how this is all going to turn out. I want to see if we can really handle this. It might not be bad, and it might suffice to make us a stronger couple. I believe that would be wonderful."

"Or it could just drive a wedge between us and make us realize that we should not have done this. It could break us up. Make us realize that we just don't want to be together anymore."

"Well, I guess we will just have to cross that bridge when we get to it, now, won't we?"

"Guess so, but if it doesn't work out in the end, remember this was all your idea," Carl said.

"It takes two to tango, Sir. You remember that," Kimberly said.

"Why do you have to be so hostile about it? That's always been a part of our problems; you always take life too seriously."

"Life is serious, Carl. The problem is that you don't take it serious enough."

"Oh, I take it serious enough for both of us, but I believe in having a little fun along the way. Everything can't be all serious all the time."

"And life is more than just fun and games. I am so tired of you judging me, Carl. You act like you are so innocent. It's your cheating and uncaring behavior that's turned our relationship into the fiasco that it is."

"I don't agree but you have the right to your own opinion, Kim."

"You don't have to agree. That's your prerogative."

"Look, I'm not the only person that cheated in this relationship. You aren't all that innocent yourself."

"I only cheated to get back at you. So, you would know how it felt."

"Say whatever you want, Kim. Cheating is cheating. I don't care why you say you did it. Cheating is cheating."

"One time doesn't compare to the many times that you did it, Carl. And I can't believe you made such a big deal about it after all the torture that you put me through."

"Cheating in my book is unforgivable," he said.

"Are you serious? Unforgivable? If that were the case, then why would you do it so many times and then beg me to forgive you all those times. I mean, you actually made me feel bad for even considering ending this shamble of a relationship."

"I said it was unforgivable for me. You have to make up your own mind. You decided to forgive me. I would not have forgiven you all those times."

"That's a double standard, Carl and you know it."

"No, it's a personal standard. You have to set your own personal boundaries on what you will tolerate. I would not tolerate you cheating on me all those times. The fact that you forgave me does not have any bearing on my views of it."

"You are unbelievable. I can't do this with you right now. I got to get out of here. I can't believe this. All of the things that I have done and sacrifice for you and you say what you've just said to me. Do you even care about my feelings? Do they cross your mind when you formulate the thoughts in your head?"

"Stop asking stupid questions, Kim. You know I care about your feelings. I'm just saying that some things in life are deal breakers. Cheating on me is one of those things."

"So why are we still together, Carl? Why are we even here, about to do this open marriage thing? I cheated on you, and you said you could never forgive it, so why even try?"

"You want the truth? It's because I know that you didn't really cheat on me. I know that you were just trying to teach me a lesson and it backfired on you. I'm still here because I hope you learned your lesson when you realized how close you came to losing me. I know you love me, and I know that you will do anything for me, so why not just let you show me. I love you too and that's why I'm still here. Yes, it's been a little hard when I picture someone else touching you but, I'm looking past it because I know it was staged."

"Unfathomable. You are impossible and I can't be in the same room with you right now," Kimberly said as she walked up the stairs and out of the basement.

3 REALIZATIONS

When Kimberly arrived at the top of the basement stairs, she slammed the basement door behind her as she exited. She stormed into the powder room that was directly across the hall, also slamming that door. She closed the lid on the toilet seat and sat down. She needed to be alone to calm down and collect her thoughts. She could not believe some of the things that Carl had just said to her. She knew that he was a bit self-centered, but she always thought that she was the exception to a lot of his views. Kimberly never thought that he saw her just as he saw the rest of the world. The thought of this brought a sense of betrayal over her. Here she was doing things to save her marriage and to keep her husband and here he was capitalizing on her sacrifices. It was the coldest and most inconsiderate thing that she had ever witnessed.

Kimberly began to feel stupid in her decision to consider this open relationship thing. How could she go to such lengths to save her marriage while her husband was only in it to enjoy himself? He was not involved to save the marriage or to ensure that they both had what they needed to be happy in the relationship. It seemed that the relationship was the least of his worries. He did not care whether he was with her or not. He'd merely found a way to sleep with other women and here she was not only condoning his horrible behavior but joining in with it.

Kimberly did not recognize this part of herself. Since she had been married to Carl, she had become a different woman. Her tolerance and standards had been lowered. Before she met him, she would never have tolerated any of the things that he had done to her. The difference with him was that she really loved him, and she was married to him. In her vows, she said she would love him for better or for worse. She just figured that this was one of those "worse" situations. She did not know that he would ever use her love against her. Carl was also the father of her children and she wanted to have him there. She could not imagine her children growing up without him. After all, he really was a great father when he was around.

Kimberly took a deep breath. She thought about the rendezvous that they had planned for the next few hours. How could she go through with having sex with another man while her husband was in the house, all while knowing that he was doing the exact same thing with another woman at the same time? Did she really believe that this would be best for their marriage? She realized that Carl did not care anymore about who touched her. He said he could not get over being cheated on, yet he said he only forgave her because he knew that the act was staged, but it wasn't. Yes, she had sex with another man to get back at her husband, but she did enjoy it just the same. She would have never done it if she were not trying to get back at him. If he forgave her, that means that he should not be able to deal with someone else touching her, yet he was totally okay with this opening of the marriage. Maybe, he hasn't forgiven her and is just saying that he has so she would allow him to be with other women. Maybe he was using her as a sacrifice to be promiscuous. Or maybe he didn't love her. Maybe he doesn't care about her anymore, which makes it easy for him to allow another man to be with her. Whichever the reason, it was too much for Kimberly to deal with and she knew that she needed to do something about it. But what could she do? She had already made her bed and must now lie in it.

With her head in her hands, Kimberly began to cry uncontrollably. She did not know how her life had become what it was. When did she stoop so low that she let a man take her self-worth? How could she not care enough about herself to put a stop to this whole situation and relationship? Why could she not just walk away from it all? After all that Carl had just admitted to her, was she still considering going through with this craziness? Was it that part of her was curious to see what it was all about? Did she really crave the touch of another man? It had been weeks since Carl touched her. She did miss being made to feel like a woman. It was all too much to bear, and the burden was heavy.

After a few minutes, Kimberly's tears slowed down, and she wiped her eyes. She stood up and looked in the mirror over the stink. She turned on the water and splashed it on her face. After she dried it with the towel that hung on a hook nearby, she gained her composure. She decided that she would go through this grand act of the opening of her relationship, but she would no longer do it for him. She would do it for herself and the outcome in reference to their relationship would just have to be dealt with when the time arose. If Carl wasn't going to be worried about it or her, then she wouldn't worry about any of it either.

Kimberly took a deep breath, straightened her clothes, and exited the bathroom. She walked back over to the basement door, paused for a second and took a deep breath. She opened the door and descended the stairs. Carl was still sitting on the couch watching television.

"You get yourself together?" He asked over his shoulder as she approached.

"Absolutely," she replied.

"Good, we can't have all of this emotional stuff going on when they get here."

"You are absolutely right," Kimberly said.

"Okay then, so which room do you want?"

"I don't care. I'll figure it out when he gets here."

"Well, I'm staying down here in the man cave."

"Whatever, Carl. I really don't care what you do. Maybe we'll stay down here too. Make it a regular orgy."

"Whatever floats your boat," Carl said.

"Unbelievable," Kimberly said. "Unbelievable."

"Why do you keep saying that?" He asked.

"Because I can't believe that you say some of the things that come out of your mouth."

"I don't understand what is so surprising for you. I'm just being honest. Isn't that the way it's supposed to be?"

"Yes, if you put it that way but, you don't have to be brutally honest all the time."

"Well, I like it this way. Nothing to hide."

"Well, I believe it might be a day late and dollar short. Maybe if we were honest like this from the beginning, we wouldn't be in this mess."

"What mess? Why do you keep saying that? When did this become a mess?"

"It has always been a mess, Carl. I mean let's look at this thing for what it is. We are about to open our relationship. We are about to let others into our bed. We are about to condone letting our significant others sleep around. I would say that that is mess."

"I don't see it as mess. I see it as two mature adults making a conscious decision to live the way they want regardless of what society thinks," Carl says.

"That's just a cop-out way of looking at it. You just need an excuse to have an open relationship."

"Whatever, Kim. Just like I said earlier, this was your idea. You came up with this mess, as you like to call it, so live with it. You made the bed, so sleep in it and be quiet about it."

"You know, I might have made the bed, but you built the house that houses the bed."

"Okay, so here we go talking in circles. Didn't we just have this conversation? Feel free to walk out of this at any time. Like I said, we don't have to do this. There are always other alternatives."

"We tried the other alternatives, remember. None of them worked."

"There's one that we haven't tried. Just say the word."

"We are not breaking up, Carl. Unless that's what you want."

Kimberly paused because there was a part of her that still feared that he no longer wanted to be with her. She still could not bring herself to accept the idea of ending her marriage. She knew that they could get through whatever their problems were if they just worked at it. She also could not deal with or accept the idea that underneath it all, he didn't want to be with her.

"I didn't say that I wanted to break up. Believe me; if I didn't want to be here, I would have left two years ago when you told me what you did. It would have been a great reason to get the hell out of dodge right at that time," he said.

"When I did what I did? Wow, that's priceless. Do you have any idea the kind of hurt you've inflicted on me? Have you ever thought about how much you've done to make me feel like crap?"

"I know that I hurt you a few times, but not to a point where you couldn't get over it."

"Not to a point where I couldn't get over it? Are you kidding me? Do you need me to refresh your memory?"

"Uh, no Kimberly, I was there. I know what happened."

"Do you? Do you really know what happened? Carl, I was in the hospital having your baby. I was in labor for 36 hours before they finally decided to do a C-section. Where were you for the bulk of those hours? When they wheeled me into the operating room for the delivery, where were you? You let me go through all of that by myself, just so you could be with some skank at an amusement park, so you could have sex. When you finally did show up, you lied about losing your wallet and not being able to get any gas to get there. Seriously, that's got to sound like the dumbest thing that I've ever heard. Doesn't it sound crazy to you?"

"It wasn't just for sex. I wasn't ready to be a father, so I didn't know how to handle it. I couldn't bring myself to be there. I didn't know what else to do."

"So, you just left me there by myself?"

"You were fine. Your mother and sister were there."

"My mother and sister didn't lay-up with me and make that baby, Carl."

"Well, it all worked out in the end. You were fine and so was CJ."

"With no thanks from you."

"Oh well, it's too late now. It's not like we can go back and change it so, why even talk about it."

"I notice that you never want to talk about things that involve you doing the wrong thing."

"Because it's in the past and there's nothing that we can do about it now. It's stupid to just keep rehashing all of this mess."

"Oh, so now you're calling it mess?"

"Not this that we're doing today. The stuff in the past was mess."

"So, you are the authority on what is classified as mess now?"

"Kim, I'm really not in the mood to be talking about our relationship and how we got to where we are. I mean, what difference does it make how we got here. The point is this is where we are now. We need to learn to live with it or not, but there should be no regrets. If you regret, that means you have shame and guilt. I don't have either, so let's move on."

"Well, I'm happy that you don't have any. My life is loaded with the stuff."

Shame and guilt were the main words to define Kimberly's life at the moment. She had nothing but remorse and regret for her past decisions. She wished that her esteem granted her the access to make more solid decisions, but instead, she did whatever she thought was necessary to keep her husband happy and in the relationship. None of her decisions were for her personal fulfillment. She was only trying to please him and give him what she thought would keep him.

"I don't know why your life is loaded with it. Maybe you should look into the decisions that you make. You might be a bit happier."

"That's easier said than done, Carl."

"No, it's not. You see what you want to do and then you go and do it. If other people don't like it, then exclude them from your inner circle. That's what I do. I only associate with people that can help me better myself. No one gets to use me for his or her own personal betterment. That's just foul on so many different levels."

"Carl, I make it a point to ensure that you have everything you need from me as your wife. Sometimes it doesn't make me happy, but I do it anyway because I promised to do it when I married you. It's called sacrifice and compromise."

"There's compromise and then there's conformity. I don't conform for anyone. You should try that."

"So, you're saying I shouldn't have changed anything about myself for you either?"

"No, I'm not saying that. I'm just saying that you are the main person that lives with you, so if you decide to change who you are, you should at least be happy with whomever you become."

"Sounds good in theory, Carl, but real life doesn't always work like that. Women have been compromising for centuries. They don't just do it for the husbands. They do it for their parents, their children, and anyone else who depends on them in the maternal and spousal roles."

"Well, that's ridiculous. There comes a time when you have to take care of yourself because no one else is going to. Not to mention, no one knows how to take care of me better than me."

"Sometimes it's not necessary to be so self-focused, especially if you have someone that you love who is willing to take care of you. I mean, you take care of each other. Isn't that what love and marriage are all about?"

"That's what fairy tale love is. That's not realistic, Kim. I mean, look at all that we've been through. Don't you think that it's time that you give up on the fantasy?"

"No, I will not. Just because you don't believe in unconditional love doesn't mean that it doesn't exit, Carl."

"Well, my perception is my reality. I can only live in my own reality. I can't live the one that you want me to live, Kim. Why are we talking about this anyway? We are supposed to be feeling loose. I mean, we are about to open our relationship. It shouldn't be all tense in here like this. You shouldn't be crying; you should be anticipating the good feelings that you are about to have."

"I guess I'm not looking at this situation the way that you are. I'm not all overjoyed about inviting people over just to have sex to commemorate the opening of our relationship."

"Well, I am. I am highly motivated about starting this thing and it's not just about the sex."

"Sure, it's about the sex, Carl. That's what it's always about for you."

"No, it's not. It's about us finally being able to relax and not having to walk around on eggshells. That's going to be the best part of the whole thing. I'm hoping that we can reach a point where we can talk about any and everything without judgment or animosity."

"I don't know if we will ever get there, Carl."

"I think we can do it, but like I said earlier. You will just have to loosen up. This doesn't have to be as serious as we're making it. We don't have to keep discussing how we got here and who did what to whom. We can simply choose to enjoy this moment and to take anything after it one day at a time. No expectations."

"Whatever you say, Carl. I need a drink."

"Really, when did you start drinking?" He laughed.

"Carl, you know I drink occasionally. I just don't do it often, but right now, I feel like I need to release some stress."

"Okay, well, if you really need a drink, I'll fix you one. Maybe that's what we both need so we can loosen up and relax. We don't want those guys to show up and we are all uptight. Yes, a drink might be just what the doctor ordered.

"Oh, so I guess that means you're going to take one with me?"

"No one wants to drink alone. Misery loves company."

"Misery, huh?"

"Of course. Not to mention, I can't just leave you out there flapping by yourself."

"Oh well, thanks for nothing. I think."

татата MONTGOMERY

4 HAPPIER TIMES

Kimberly watched as Carl created two drinks using scotch and cranberry juice. He made her drink a bit smaller than his and added more juice. When he was done, he handed her the glass.

"Toast?" He asked.

"Sure," she said reluctantly. "What do we toast to?"

"Whatever you want."

"I don't know. Let's toast to making it through some really tough times."

"Okay, let's do it."

"Yes, to making it through and still making through right now."

"Aw come on, it's not that bad. At least we are here to toast. It might be messed up right now, but it hasn't always been this way. We used to have some great times. Our life used to be fun," Carl said, holding his glass out toward her to toast.

"You're right. It wasn't always bad,"

Kimberly said as she clinked her glass against his. "We used to have fun all the time. Even when we were not doing much of anything."

"I know. We used just sit around with each other and laugh all night."

"I used to wonder to myself in those days how could things ever go wrong between us. What could we possibly ever have to fight about?"

"I did too. It was perfect."

"You remember how we used to take walks in the middle of the night and stare up into the sky at the stars and the moon?" Kimberly asked.

"Yeah, and then come back and have sex in the car."

"Really," Kimberly laughed. "Is that all you remember?"

"No, I remember all of it, but the sex was always the best part for me."

"Is there ever a time when you don't have sex on the brain."

"Never, especially not back then. I used to think about different ways to do you even when I was already doing you. I mean, I would constantly be thinking about new ways to please you."

"You know there were other ways to please me outside of new sexual positions."

"I'm quite sure there were but the sex always adds a little extra oomph to anything that you already do."

"I'm mad that you actually believe that," Kimberly said.

"I'm mad that you don't," Carl laughed.

"But weren't those old days fun whether they ended in sex or not."

"Yeah, they were okay."

"I remember wanting to be with you all the time. I just could not get enough of you. I just wanted to spend all my time around you."

"You say that in past tense. That means you don't want to be around me like that anymore."

"Well, Carl, you aren't the nicest person anymore and it's not like we've been on the best of terms in the longest time. Hell, not to mention, you don't want to be around me like that anymore either."

"It's not that I don't want to be around you; I just can't tolerate all of the nagging and harassing."

"Is that how you see me, a nag?"

"Sometimes."

"Why? I just want what's best for you and our children. That's all. There's nothing behind anything that I say to you.

"I highly doubt that sometimes, but even if there isn't anything behind what you say, I don't need you to be my mother. You don't have to make sure that I'm doing the right thing all time. You have your own children to raise and send in the right direction. I'm already grown, and I don't need your guidance."

"You're right, you are grown and I'm not trying to give you guidance. I want to give you support and that's how I interpret what I do. There used to be a point in our relationship when you valued my opinion."

"Kim, I still value your opinion, but I don't need it all the time, every day. After a while, it just feels judgmental. You make me feel like I can't do anything right and like I need to get your approval on anything that I'm thinking even before I attempt it."

"Carl, I'm sorry. I really don't want you to feel that way. I'm just trying to make sure that you know in your heart that I am here for you. Always in your corner."

"But, why do you have to make sure I know it. That's not your place to make sure I know it. You just have to be who are and if I can't see that you love and support me, then maybe I don't deserve to be with you."

Carl's last statement sent a chill up Kimberly's back. Was he trying to say that he didn't want to be with her? Was he trying to find an excuse for them to break up?

"So, are you trying to say that you don't want to be with me? That you don't believe that I'm here for you one hundred percent?"

"No, I'm not saying that. I was just speaking

in general. If someone can't appreciate you for who you are, then they are not worthy of being in your life. You need to be able to recognize that for yourself, Kim. That's all I'm saying."

"Well, I believe that you are worthy of being in my life, so that's why I'm constantly fighting for us and our relationship. Our kids deserve to have their father as well."

"Kimberly, it's not whether or not you believe I should be worthy of being with you. It's about your self-worth. Are you worthy of yourself?"

"What? What kind of stupid question is that? You know, Carl, for you to be so intelligent. Sometimes you say some of the silliest things?"

"And for you to be so loving, you are so hateful when it comes to yourself."

"What does that mean?"

"I hate having these womanly conversations. This is girl talk. You know, the kind of stuff that they talk about with Oprah and Iyanla Vanzant. I mean, I don't watch those things all the time, but on the few shows that I did catch. I understand when they say it starts with you. That's all I'm saying."

"What?" You are losing me Carl."

"Kim, all I'm saying is that our relationship was better in the past because you were in a better place. You were more confident and self-compassionate. You didn't put yourself down and you didn't play second place to no one."

"Yes, but that was before we got married and started having kids."

"I don't understand your point," he said.

"When you are single with no children, you can stay focused on yourself. You don't have to worry about anyone else. Once you start having babies, you realize that you have this other life in your hands that you have to mold and shape. It's hard to stay focused on yourself. Not to mention, it's selfish. You can't be self-centered when you have this new being that is trying to learn to navigate its way through the world. That would be mean for me to let my child grow without helping him learn the ways of life."

"Kimberly, no one told you to neglect your children, but you don't have to neglect yourself to be a good mom."

"Carl, you have no idea what it means to be a mother. It's hard and time-consuming. And you worry constantly about your children. You take it personal the type of people that they grow up to be. You realize that the things they do and don't do are a direct reflection of yourself."

"So, are you saying that I am not a parent? Last time I checked, we shared the same two children."

"No, that's not what I'm saying at all. It's

just different for mothers, that's all. And wives."

"It's not different for wives. They fool themselves into thinking that it is, which is why relationships have so many problems. I think a lot of women have a hard time deciphering between their role as a mother and as a wife. They are not the same and the husband shouldn't be seen as one of the children."

"Carl, I've never seen you as one of my children but, I do see you as someone that I love and need to take care of."

"I appreciate that, but I don't need you to take care of me, Kim. I'm a grown man and I can do that for myself. Plus, you shouldn't be taking care of me at the expense of losing yourself."

"I haven't lost myself, Carl. What a mean thing to say?"

"I'm not trying to be mean, but you have lost yourself. When is the last time that you've done anything for yourself. Anything that you enjoy doing? When is the last time you danced or sang a song? When I met you, you used to love to do those things all the time."

"It's not that I don't think about doing those things. I think about it all the time. I just don't have time like I used to. There are too many things to get done throughout the course of a day. I have to go to work. Help the kids with their schoolwork, cook dinner, and clean the house. You know a woman's work is never done," she laughed, trying to lighten up the conversation.

"Those all sound like excuses. I find time to do the things I love to do, and I work too."

"Yes Carl, but you are not as involved with the kids like I am. And I'm not saying that to sound mean."

"I know what you mean but you can find time if you want to."

"I try to find time to be with you as well. Even that's hard. I love spending time with you. I always have."

Carl did not respond to her last statement. He took a deep breath and carried his drink back over to the couch. Kimberly followed, carry her drink as well.

"Carl, don't you like spending time with me anymore?"

"I do, but just not every waking minute. Plus, you know our relationship is not what it used to be. We aren't the same people. We've been through a lot."

"I know and that's what I'm trying to fix. We can be what we were if you just believed it, Carl."

"I loved who we were, but I know that was a different place and different time. I've accepted the fact that we are probably never going to get back to that."

"Well, I haven't. I know we can be, but we just have to be willing to put in the same effort that we did back then."

"The feelings aren't the same, Kim."

"But they can be, Carl."

"No, they can't be. I don't trust you anymore and from the looks of things. You don't trust me either."

"You don't trust me? Why not?"

"Kim, you cheated on me."

"Carl, I cheated on you out of spite. There was nothing to that. I only got with someone else so you could see how it felt to be betrayed and lied to."

"Well, mission accomplished. I know what it feels like and it's hard for me to let it go."

"Look, Carl, I don't want to go back down this road in this conversation. Why can't we or should I say you, just move past this. I mean, we decided that we are going to stay together, so you have to start trusting eventually. There's no relationship without trust."

"I agree and that's why I'm hoping our little rendezvous that's about to happen in the next hour and a half will help to manage this situation," Carl said, looking at the watch on his wrist.

"Carl, there was a time when you loved me so much that you would never consider letting another man talk to me, more or less put his hands on me."

"That was a different time, Kim. You already gave me an image of you with another man when you cheated. Before, I couldn't imagine it. Now that I have the image in my head, it's all that I see when I see you or think of being intimate with you. I can't shake it. It makes it hard for me to love you the way that I used to. All I can see is the guy inside you, in my personal space. It's never going to be the same."

"Carl," Kimberly said as tears rolled down her face. "You let someone into my personal space as well. It's hard for me to get that image out of my head as well, but I know how to look past it to love you unconditionally and in spite of."

"Well, I guess that makes you a better person than me."

"I don't want to be better than you. I want us to be equals. That's what makes for a great relationship and marriage."

"We aren't equal, Kim. You hurt me and from what I know, you did it intentionally."

"You hurt me too, Carl."

"Yes, but it was never my intent to hurt you. I never considered hurting you in any of the things that I did."

"Just because you didn't mean to doesn't

mean that you didn't know that you would. You never considered my feelings in any of your decisions and from where I stand, that makes you just as guilty as I am."

"We are never going to see eye to eye on this. You just need to know that it's hard for me to forgive you. I have already stepped out of my normal behavior by still being in this marriage. Normally, I would walk away the instant that I found out. I'm trying to push past it for the sake of our children, but it's hard. That's why I'm willing to give this open marriage thing a try."

"I think you're only doing it so you can just have sex with different women without the guilt."

"You would think that. But have you ever stopped to think that I can just walk away and have sex without guilt? Why would I need to stay in a relationship to have sex with other women?"

"Because then you lose your kids."

"No, my kids will always be my kids. I'll never lose them. Unless you're trying to tell me something."

"I'm not trying to tell you anything. I'm just saying, that's all."

"Look, Kim. I love you. That's why I'm still here. I know that might be hard for you to understand but I do. It's hard for me to see you the same because I feel betrayed, but I still love you, which is why I'm still here. I'm just tired of the way we are living and I'm open to something new. Something that might help to make this all better. To put a smile on my face and yours. Lord, knows I don't know how to make you smile anymore."

Kimberly was touched by Carl's last statement. She was not sure if he still loved her, and he just confirmed it. She was also touched that he still wanted to make her smile. That she was still important enough for him to think of her smile at all.

"Carl, all you have to do is be here with me. Be a part of me."

"Kim, I can't right now. I can't get past all the cheating stuff. Maybe I will in the future, but it's just too much for me. You have to give me time."

"I don't know what to say to that."

"Don't say anything, just accept it. Give me time and space."

"Space? What kind of space?"

"I don't know. Just space. Just let me be. I will live by the rules of this open relationship that we came up with earlier. Other than that, we have to just take one day at a time with no expectations."

"It sounds like you want to have your cake and eat it too."

"No, I just want the opportunity to realize that there is a cake, Kim."

"Now you're talking in riddles, Carl and I have no idea what you mean?"

"Me either. I don't know what I mean. Let's just sit here and wait for them to get here. Maybe we should stop talking," he said, taking a sip of his drink.

"Okay, Carl. Whatever you say. I'll stop talking to you. I need to go call Cindy to check up on the kids anyway."

"Cindy? The kids are with Cindy?"

"Yes, Carl. You knew that already."

"No, I didn't. I thought that they were with your mother."

"Okay, well, they're with Cindy. What's the big deal?"

"Uh, nothing. It's not a big deal. I was just surprised, that's all. I have never seen you leave them with her overnight."

"Well, she said she could do it when I asked, so it all worked out."

"Okay, that's fine," he said nervously.

"Carl, what the hell is wrong with you."

"Nothing, you go ahead and check on the kids. I'm chilling."

Kimberly stared at him for a few seconds. He seemed to get really nervous all of a sudden. She knew that there was something that he was not telling her. She turned and headed up the stairs to the kitchen, where she left her cell phone on the island. What was he not telling her? Why did it make a difference that the kids were with Cindy and not her mother? Things just got strange. Cindy has been babysitting for them for the past seven years since Kimberly had her first baby. There was no reason for him to be surprised. What the hell was going on?

PART TWO

5 THINGS IN THE GAME DONE CHANGED

Carl waited until Kimberly reached the top of the stairs and exited the basement. He made sure that the door was closed and then reached into his pocket for his cell phone. He searched for Cindy's number and sent her a text message.

You have my children?

He took a sip from his drink as he waited for Cindy's response. He stared at the phone.

Yes, Cindy responded.

Why? He asked.

Because she asked me to keep them.

Why did you say yes?

Why wouldn't I?

Because you're supposed to be coming here. How can you keep the kids if you're supposed to be here in a little while?

Don't worry about it. I got it worked out.

Explain

My niece is going to stay with them.

Why didn't you just say no?

Because then I would have had to tell her why I couldn't do it.

No, you didn't.

Carl waited for a response. There was none.

He stood up from the couch and paced the room. Cindy was playing things a little too close. She was supposed to be coming to the house to be a part of the opening ceremony, as he liked to call it. He knew that Kimberly would be mad when she realized that he had chosen Cindy as his first quest, but he had been flirting with her since they met seven years earlier. This was a perfect opportunity for him to finally take it to the next level.

After a few minutes, Cindy sent another message.

Quit worrying. I have it under control. I just got off the phone with her.

Don't mess this up. I really want to see you.

I know you do and don't worry.

Okay, see you soon, he said.

He placed his phone back in his pocket just as Kimberly opened the basement door and came back down the stairs.

"The kids are fine. They are making cookies with Cindy's niece Tiara."

"Okay, that's good."

"So why did you get so nervous when I told you that they were with Cindy," Kimberly asked.

"I wasn't nervous. I was just surprised. I know you don't usually let them stay out overnight with just anyone. It was just different. That's all."

"Cindy has kept them overnight before, Carl."

"Yes, but only in our house."

"Does it make a difference?"

"Nope. You are the one that's making a big deal about it."

"I'm not making a big deal about it. I just noticed that you started acting really strange as soon as I mentioned Cindy's name, that's all."

"I said I wasn't acting strange or nervous. I told you what was going on. So, stop it, Kim. You're starting to piss me off. I'm trying to stay cool for today. Let's not do this."

"Let's not do what, Carl?"

"I'm done, Kim. Nothing else to talk about in reference to this."

Carl pulled his phone from his pocket and opened his Facebook app in hopes that she would catch the hint and let it go. He scrolled through his newsfeed as if he was totally engrossed in what he was doing. He could feel her eyes on his back as she stood over him.

"Whatever, Carl," she said after a few moments.

Carl said nothing, continuing to read the posts on his newsfeed.

"So, what now?" Kim asked.

"What do you mean?"

"What do we do until they get here? You said you didn't want to talk. So, what do we do now?"

"I never said I didn't want to talk. I just didn't see why we needed to argue about Cindy and the kids."

"Uh huh. Okay, fine."

"Okay, fine."

Carl reached for one of the sidearm pillows on the couch, sat back and put the pillow behind his head. He placed his phone face down on his stomach and closed his eyes. He thought about how much of a scene it was going to be when Kimberly realized that it was Cindy that he had chosen for this opening thing. He did not know how he was going to defuse the situation and it had him worried.

"What are you thinking about?" Kim asked.

"Nothing. Just trying to relax."

"I'm happy that you can relax because that's the furthest thing from my mind."

"You know, it doesn't have to be that way."

"I don't know how to make it any other way, Carl."

"You can just let go of this idea of what our relationship should be and accept it for what it really is," Carl said not opening his eyes.

"It amazes me how you are so smug."

Carl ignored her last comment. He was not smug. He was a bit nervous and anxious. He was excited to finally be able to get with Cindy. All these things were playing in his mind, and it was enough to make him curious to know how it would all turn out. There would be no going back. He refused to let Kimberly change her mind. He needed to be able to see this thing through to the end. If things didn't proceed and continue after this first act, then he would cross that bridge when they got to it, but this had to happen today. Also, it would help him to decide if staying in this marriage was worth it. Right now, he could really think of no other reason to move forward with it.

"So, where are you going to take your friend?" He asked.

"I haven't decided yet," Kimberly said.

"Oh, well, you have your choice of areas. I mean it's not like the kids are here and I won't be coming out of the basement to see anyway."

"I don't know if I want him in any other part of my house. I don't want him to get it confused."

"He's a man. I promise he won't get it confused. Did you tell him what we were doing?"

"Well yes and no."

"What does that mean?"

"I told him that we were opening, but I

didn't tell him that you would be here when he got here. Did you tell your friend?"

"Yes, she knows that you're going to be here. I figured it was only right, so she won't get nervous when she sees."

"How considerate of you."

"I try," Carl said. "I mean, what other way could it have been done?"

"I don't know. I guess I should be thankful. It does cut down on the discomfort level for all of us. So, are you going to be able to handle this?"

"Handle what?"

"Seeing the man that you know is going to be having sex with me, right before he does it?"

"Who said I was going to see him."

"Well, I just figured we would answer the door together when they arrived."

"Oh, I hadn't thought about it."

"Well, if we did, that would save us from having to discuss who they are. We can just introduce them and go about our business."

"Okay, sounds good to me," Carl said. He knew that would be the exact opposite of what would happen once Kim saw that it was Cindy at the door.

"So, you never answered my question," Kim said.

"What was the question again," he asked, finally opening his eyes.

"I said are you going to be okay with seeing the man that you know is about to have sex with me."

"Kim, I see the man that's already had sex with you every time I look at you, so I don't think that this will be any different."

"Wow, that was mean."

"I'm sorry but it's the truth."

"Sometimes you don't always have to say what's on your mind. A simple yes would have sufficed."

"Oh well. Sorry. I need another drink," he said, rising from the couch. "How about you?"

Carl noticed that she no longer had her drink in her hand.

"Where is your drink?" He asked.

"Oh, I took it upstairs when I went to call Cindy. I guess I forgot to bring it back down."

"Do you want another one? Did you finish it?"

"No, I didn't finish it but, I don't feel like going back upstairs to get it either."

"So does that mean that you want another one?" He asked as he poured himself another drink.

"Yes, please and make it just like yours. I don't want the weak little-girl-drink this time."

"You sure you can handle it? I don't want you to be sleeping before they get here. You can't be drunk."

"I can handle it," Kimberly said.

"Okay, whatever you say."

"Maybe I need to be drunk, so this won't be so serious for me. Maybe it will help relax my inhibitions."

"No man wants to be with a drunk woman. Not a real man. We need you aware, so you can be just as involved as we are."

"Oh really?"

"Yes really. No one wants a limp noodle, Kim."

"A limp noodle," she laughed. "That would have to be on his part. I don't have a noodle."

"You know what I mean," he laughed.

"I thought men liked to take advantage."

"They like to dominate but not rape the woman."

"Oh, I see."

"Come on now, you know this."

"I know that you used to like it when I was a little tipsy. It was easier for you to convince me to do things that I didn't normally do."

"Notice you said a little tipsy. Not inebriated."

"Okay, I got it," she laughed. "Just make the drink."

"Yes Ma'am."

There was an awkward moment of silence between them. Carl felt like he should say something, except nothing would come to his mind. He wanted to keep the situation and conversation light, but he was not sure of how to accomplish it. He looked at her and smiled.

"What are you smiling at?" Kim asked.

"I like when you're like this. You are fun when you aren't stressing."

"Thank you. I want to be fun."

"So do it."

"I'm trying. Don't make me start thinking again."

"Okay, so you want to shoot a game of pool?" He asked, pointing to his pool table on the other side of the room.

"Yeah, I think I can find the time and stamina to bust you up right fast," Kimberly said.

"Well, let's get it," he said, handing her the drink that he had just made for her. He walked out of the bar area and headed over to the pool table.

"Don't take this ass whipping personal," Kimberly stuttered.

"Oh, so now you're doing movie quotes?" Carl laughed.

"You know Harlem Nights is one of my favorites."

"Yeah, I know, so you won't take it personal when you lose."

"Bring it on buddy," Kim said. "I'll even let you break."

"Well, how nice of you, but you know it's always lady's first," he said, grabbing the triangle from under the table.

"Okay, but I tried to help you get a head start."

"That's all right. I'm a big boy. I can handle myself."

"We shall see."

"Yes, we shall," he said as he began to rack the balls into the triangle.

"Make sure it's a good rack," Kim said. "I don't want you making excuses when I sink the eight ball on the break."

"What? Wishful thinking, but I'll make sure it's tight for you."

"Well, thank you so much, Sir."

Kimberly grabbed one of the three pool sticks that Carl kept near the table. He watched as she put chalk on the end of the stick. He removed the triangle from the balls and placed it back underneath the table.

"Here we go," Kimberly said.

She poised herself over the table and hit the cue ball with a bit of force. Carl watched as the balls scattered around the table and as the eight ball rolled into the right corner pocket.

"You have got to be kidding me," he laughed. "Talk about dumb luck."

"That is not dumb luck. I warned you," Kim gloated.

"Wow, you know that was luck."

"I'm just that good. You keep underestimating me."

"No, I know that you are good, just not at pool. That was just some dumb luck."

"Whatever, just re-rack it so I can do it again."

"Alright, we'll see," he said, grabbing all of the balls again. He liked that she was laughing and smiling. Maybe, it would make the situation easier when she laid eyes on Cindy. Maybe it wouldn't make a difference. Maybe he could keep her so happy that she won't care who shows up at the front door. And maybe she won't make a big deal about Cindy leaving the kids with someone else. Okay, he knew that the last part of that thought was wishful thinking. Maybe, he needed to convince Cindy to take the kids to his mother's house, but then he knew that would just make Kim angrier. He would have to not only convince Cindy, but he would have to do it within the next hour before it was time for them to arrive. That would mean that he would have to get in touch with Cindy again without Kim knowing it. Carl had no idea how he would get Kim out of the room so he could contact Cindy. Not to mention, he did not think it was wise to change the atmosphere at this moment. He finished racking the balls and stepped back from the table.

"You ready?" Kim smiled.

"And you know it. Let me see you do it again," he said.

"Okay, watch and pay attention, young buck," she said.

"Oh, I'm watching and I'm definitely paying attention," Carl said.

6 MORE OF THE SAME

Carl opened his eyes and stared at the two women standing before him. He could not believe what he had just heard. Did she really just say what he thought that she had just said? His ears had to be misleading him. There's no way that she said what he thinks.

"What did you just say?" He asked Cindy.

"I said I'm not here for you; I'm here for Kim."

"You mean you are here to see Kim about the kids, right?"

"No, I'm here to do with Kim; what you think I came to do with you?"

"I think you just came here to have sex with me and you're saying that you came here to have sex with Kimberly."

"Yes, Carl. That's exactly what she's saying," Kimberly said.

"You're kidding right?"

"Nope," Cindy said.

"How can you be here for her?"

"Because I couldn't go through with what you were trying to do. She's a woman and we have to stick together."

"So, you told her about us?"

"Yes, because there is no us and there never will be."

"Yes Carl, this is what happens when you try to get over on people. Now you get to see how it feels," Kim added.

"So, what about your friend?" Carl asked.

"He's coming too. It's going to be a threesome."

"Wait what? And what about me?"

"What about you?" The two women said in unison.

Carl blinked and looked around. He couldn't believe what he had just heard. He stared at the television that was playing in front of him. This was when he realized that he had been dreaming. After, he played another round of pool with Kim, who beat him again; he went and sat back on the couch. Kim said she had to use the bathroom. He did not know how long he had been asleep, and the dream felt so real. He did not realize that the idea of Cindy as a part of the grand opening was messing with him as much as it had. He needed to get this thing worked out because it was now invading his dreams. Was he really this worried about it? Or did he want to see both women together? Was that what he wished for underneath it all? It had not dawned on him before the dream, but he had to admit that it would be a great surprise ending to it all.

"What are you over here thinking about?" Kim asked as she returned from the bathroom.

"Oh, I fell asleep that fast. I was trying to figure out how I did that."

"Well, it's been about ten minutes and the way you took those last two drinks to the head, I can see how you would fall asleep. Not to mention, it is kind of hot in here."

"Oh yeah, you're right. Let me go turn the heat down a little bit."

Carl stood up and walked over to the thermostat on the other side of the room. It read 78 degrees as the ambient temperature even though it was set at 75 degrees. He lowered it to seventy-four and returned to his place on the couch.

"Well, we still have about an hour before they arrive. Anything you feel like watching until then?" He asked.

"No, not really."

"Okay, well I guess we can just flick channels."

"Or we can just not watch TV. There are other things that we can do," Kim said, smiling.

"Like what?" He asked.

"I'm open to whatever you want to do, but I

think I need another drink."

"Really, I noticed that you took that one to the head. I guess it's working. You are loosening up."

"I am and it feels good."

"That's good to hear. Let me get you that drink. You want the same thing?"

"No, I think I want one of my own type of drinks this time. Maybe a Coco Loco."

"Okay, I think I can handle that. That would be Coconut Vodka and Pineapple juice, right?"

"You got it."

"Sounds good. I'm on it," he said, heading back over to the bar area of the basement.

"How about you? Are you drinking the same thing?" Kim asked as she walked over to where he was. She began rubbing her hands up and down his back.

"Yes, you know I'm a scotch man. I don't drink any of that girly stuff."

"Girly stuff, huh? I got some girly stuff for you," Kim said, putting her hand under his sweater.

Carl knew that she was trying to seduce him and as much as he wanted to give in, he did not know if this was a good idea. He wanted to be at the top of his game when he got with Cindy later. He knew that this could either make or break him. If he had an orgasm with Kimberly, it might be harder for him to get an erection when he was with Cindy later. Or the flip side would be that he got the erection and he lasted longer because he had just been with Kim. Since he wasn't sure, he did not know how to respond. He was also fighting with the thought that picturing her with someone else would make it impossible for him to perform with Kim. This has been a battle that he had been fighting since she cheated on him two years earlier. He normally had to deal with it by pretending that she was someone else and blocking out what he knew. Usually, once he got started, it was easy to turn off his mind.

He finished fixing the drinks and turned around to hand her the glass. She took it from him and drank it in one swallow.

"Wow," he said.

"Your turn," she said. "Take it to the head."

Carl turned the glass up and swallowed its entire contents.

"Nice," Kim said. She removed the glass from his hand.

"Kim," Carl said.

"Yes," she said as she rose up on her toes to kiss him.

"I don't know if this is a good idea," Carl said.

"Why not?" Kim asked, planting a light kiss on his lips.

"You know why. We are about to be with

other people."

"So, and what does that mean?"

"It means, don't you want to be ready for it?"

"I will be. One has nothing to do with the other."

Carl felt as her hand trailed down his stomach and stopped between his legs. Instantly he felt a twinge of excitement run through him.

"I just don't want to not be able to perform when the time comes."

"I'm sure you'll be just fine, Carl," she said thrusting her tongue into his mouth.

Carl wanted to fight her off, but her tongue was all it took to make him give in. He reasoned that she was right and that he would not only be able to perform but that this little encounter would only help boost his performance.

"Plus, I want to be with you one last time as only mine before I start sharing you with the rest of the world," Kim said.

"I like that idea," Carl said, unbuckling her pants.

"Do you now," she breathed.

Carl ran his tongue over her neck and then clamped his lips down around the spot where his tongue stopped. Kimberly tightened her hold on his penis and electricity shot through him again.

"Hell yeah," he said between sucks on her

neck.

He pulled her shirt over her head and unhooked her bra in one smooth motion. He then moved his mouth from her neck to her left breast.

"Oh my God," she hissed. Her hand released his pants as he bent down. "That feels so good."

"You like that?"

"Oh yes."

Carl cupped her other breast as he continued sucking like his life depended on it. It had been a while since they were together, and he realized that he missed her. He remembered that he was overjoyed with her sexually and that he could never get enough of her.

"Mmmm," he said as he moved to mouth her right nipple.

"Oh yes," she said again.

Carl placed his hands between her legs, and he could feel her wetness through her cotton panties. The feeling sent whatever blood he had left throughout his body to the head of his penis. He removed his hands and mouth from her breasts and kneeled, so his head was in line with her crotch. He put his nose against her.

"Damn, I love that smell," he said, inhaling her scent. He licked her wetness through her panties.

"Oh my God," she cried. "Take them off."

Instead, Carl took his finger and pushed the crotch section of her panties aside, exposing her wetness. He spread her labia slightly apart, exposing her clitoris. He looked up at her, hoping that this would cause a reaction. Kimberly threw her head back in anticipation of what was to happen next. Carl began to finger her clitoris with his index finger.

"Oh yes, yes, yes," she said, getting louder. Which only made Carl want to continue.

"You want my tongue on it?" He asked.

"Hell yeah," Kimberly pleaded.

Carl placed the tip of his tongue on Kimberly's clitoris, and she began to tremble. He continued to move his tongue in the area, enjoying her response.

"Oh my God, that feels so good, she said, grabbing his head.

Carl lifted her left leg to get a better angle. He held her panties further aside and pushed his tongue up inside her.

"You are going to make me cum," she screamed. "Oh my God."

Carl stopped licking her, "Not yet," he said.

He continued licking her but at a slower pace. After he felt her calm down a little as he stood up and kissed her passionately, he picked her up and sat her up on the counter, pushing her back against the wall. He slid her butt down to the edge of the counter and got back down on his knees. Next, he removed her panties. Once again, he buried his head between her legs, devouring her juices like he had been thirsty for days.

"Oh yes, Daddy. Eat it," she yelled.

"Yeah, I know you love it, he said between sucks of her clit.

"You are going to make me cum," she yelled again.

"Not yet," he said as he stood up again.

He opened his pants and pulled his penis out the top of his underwear. He then removed his shirt. He knew that Kimberly loved his abs, and he wanted her to see the full package. He watched as she stared at his body.

"Damn," she said.

"Why don't you come taste it?" he smiled and grabbed his penis at the same time.

"With pleasure," she said.

She jumped off the counter and wrapped her lips around his penis. Carl was in instant oblivion. He always loved the way she handled him.

"Damn girl, you know how to suck this dick," he moaned. "I love this shit."

Carl tried to control himself as he listened to her slurp and suck. His head fell backward as he felt her hand cup his testicles.

"Oh shit, not the balls," he said. "You know what that does to me."

"Uh huh," she moaned.

"You better stop if you don't want this to be over very quickly."

Kimberly began to suck harder. Carl could feel his climax coming quickly. He knew that if he didn't stop her, he would explode in her mouth. He grabbed her head to stop her movement.

Kimberly sucked faster.

"Oh shit," he cried. "I don't want to cum yet, Kim."

Carl continued to hold her head in his hands, but he was too weak to stop her. It felt too good and all he could think about was letting it go. Just when he was about to lose control, she stopped and stood up, sticking her tongue deep into his mouth. He kissed her back just as hard, picked her up, and carried her to the couch. He put her down in front of it and spun her around. Carl grabbed her around the waist and pushed her head forward, indicating that he wanted to enter her from behind.

"Let me get that ass doggy style," he said.

"You can get it however you want it, but I want you to finish eating me first," Kim said.

"Oh, with pleasure, he said as she turned back to face him. She sat down on the couch, laid back, lifting and spreading her legs at the same time.

Carl kneeled down in front of her and put

his tongue inside her. Kimberly quivered and moaned.

"Oh yes, that is what I need," she said. "Please don't stop."

Carl continued to lick and suck on her until her whole body began to shiver. He then focused only on her clit with his tongue as he pushed two of his fingers inside of her. Kimberly began pumping her hips in what he knew was ecstasy. He continued this way until she busted and creamed into his mouth. Carl slurped up every ounce of her juices, which only caused her to climax two more times. When he was done, he stood and positioned himself over her for his penis to have easy access.

"I told you I want that ass doggy style, didn't I?" He asked.

"Yes," she moaned.

"Then turn over and let me get it."

He watched as she flipped over, putting her butt in the air. The visual picture of her naked behind in the air was enough to make him climax without even touching her but he held it back.

"Oh, this is not going to take long at all," he said as he entered her.

He spread her cheeks as he watched his penis slide in and out of her vagina.

"Oooh, this smells so good," he groaned. He picked up his pace and pushed in as deep as he could go. He listened as she moaned louder with each of his thrust. After a few more thrust, he felt a wave come over him and he exploded into her.

"Oh shit," he yelled as he lost his rhythm and began to only be able to thrust in small strokes. After a few minutes, his body became tired and sensitive at the same time.

"Don't move," he said.

Kim laughed. "As tight as your holding on right now, I promise you that I'm going nowhere."

Carl didn't realize that his arms were wrapped around her waist, and he was holding on for dear life. He loosened his hold as he pulled out of her. He turned from her and fell back onto the couch.

"Damn, that was good as hell," he said, closing his eyes.

"It's always good when we do it," Kim replied.

"Yeah, you're right. Damn. That is one thing that we haven't' lost," Carl said.

He took a deep breath. He knew that she was a good sexual partner, which is why it was hard for him to forgive her for giving that to someone else. It was the main thing that he could not relinquish in his thoughts. Her beautiful lips wrapped around another man's penis or her pretty butt bouncing on someone else's lap. It was these visual thoughts that he could not handle. The thought of them at this moment was almost too much for him to bear. He hopped up from the couch and headed toward the bathroom.

"I'll bring you some tissue in a minute," he said over his shoulder. He walked into the bathroom.

"Don't bother," Kim said as she got up and ran up the stairs, closing the door behind her.

This was a far different scenario from the one in his dream and he did not know how he could be thinking about this after what they had just done. He was an emotional wreck and he needed to get it together within the next hour. He did not want to seem out of sorts when Cindy arrived. He needed to have his mind right when it was time for him to confront both women at the same time. They needed to know that he could handle this and that he was game to make it through, whatever the outcome.

TARA MONTGOMERY

7 REVELATIONS

Carl grabbed a hand towel from the shelf of towels that Kim kept in the bathroom for overnight guest. He cleaned himself up at the sink. He thought of what he and Kim had just done and how much he enjoyed himself. Part of him felt guilty, almost like he had taken advantage of her, and the other part realized that he missed his wife. He did not know how he had let their relationship come to what it was. He knew that his behavior and decisions played a major role in their demise. He knew that he could put a stop to the whole thing, and it was initially his intention to do so. The thing that stopped him was that Kimberly went out and cheated on him. He knew that his behavior was hurting her but, he felt like she was strong enough to bounce back from it. He knew that she loved him enough to get past it and it was only a temporary thing for him to go and be with other women.

When she cheated, it ruined him, and it

changed the rules of the game. There was no way for their relationship to recover. She had committed the ultimate betrayal. There was no reason for her to go out and find someone else. There were numerous other ways for her to let him know that she could no longer handle it. She could have just said it to him. She didn't have to show him. That was just selfish of her. It made no difference that he had done the same on numerous occasions. Women were stronger than men. They've had babies and are better able to handle pain. She should have just pushed through. Now they were in a place that he was unable to recover from and he didn't know what to do. He really did love her but, he did not know how to express that to her anymore. He didn't know if he could trust her to not run away every time her feelings are hurt. He really was lost in this whole situation. He wanted to be with Kimberly, but he really didn't know how to be. Of course, he couldn't let her know that he was confused because then he would just look weak. He needed to keep up his image of being a strong man, one that can keep his head in the worst of situations. Only punks let themselves get lost in emotions.

 He wiped his face and exited the bathroom. Kimberly had not returned yet. He wasn't sure what she was doing, but he was hoping that they could continue to keep the situation light.

He didn't need the strain that they had earlier, and he hoped that their sexual escapade didn't ruin it.

He pulled his phone out to talk to Cindy. He found her number in his contacts and hit call.

"Hello," she said after the second ring.

"Hey, I need you to take the kids to my mother."

"For what? I told you they were going to stay with my niece."

"And what are you going to tell Kim when you get here?"

"I'm going to tell her that they are here with my niece. Didn't I just say that?"

"Look, she's already going to be mad that you are here. The last thing she needs is to be worried about the kids too. She won't let this happen if you don't do this."

"I said I had it worked out. I need you to stop calling me, Carl. Stop panicking."

"Look, I really want this to happen. It has to happen. Don't you get it? I'm going to need a reason to… Never mind. I just don't want you to mess this up for me."

"Carl, nobody is going to mess up anything for you. Stop tripping. I got it together and the kids are staying here. Oh, and stop calling me. I'll text when I'm on my way," she said right before she ended the call.

Carl stared at the phone after the call was

completed. He had plans and they had to come through. He did not need anyone to ruin them for him. This thing with Cindy had to go down. It was imperative for his future. He needed Kim to allow it, which is why he fought for some of the rules that he suggested. This had to be the way things were going to work. He needed to remain in control of this situation.

The basement door opened, and Kimberly called down to him.

"Carl, I'm going to fix a sandwich. Do you want one?"

"Yeah, that's fine. I am a little hungry," he said, happy that she was still in a good mood.

"What kind do you want?" She asked.

"You can fix me whatever you fix yourself. You know how I like them. Mustard or butter."

"Okay, be down in a minute."

"All right, thanks."

Carl walked back over to the couch and picked up the remote. He turned the television to ESPN and watched the broadcast on some college football team. He didn't really pay attention to what was showing, as his mind was focused on what would be going on in the next hour. The time was winding down fast, and he was becoming anxious.

He laid his head back against the pillow that he had positioned earlier and just as he did. His phone began to ring.

"Hello," he said into the phone after sliding the answer bar over

"Dude, what's up?" said a male voice on the other side.

"What's up, Tony?" Carl said.

"Your girl, Man. She's up to something."

"What you mean?"

"She left the house yesterday and she ain't been back," Tony said.

"Where did she go?"

"I don't know man."

"What do you mean you don't know? You were supposed to be watching her. That's what I paid you for. How hard is it?"

"I was watching her, but I left to go pee in the bushes and when I came back, I guess she was gone. I didn't see her leave the house but, nobody's home."

"If you didn't see her leave, then how do you know that nobody's home?"

"There was no lights on last night and some lady was over there ringing the doorbell earlier and nobody answered."

"Dude, how could you not see her leave? She doesn't drive her car, most days, so you should have seen her walking down the street or something. How can you miss it?"

"I didn't man. She didn't walk anywhere. Maybe she went out the back or something. Maybe she knew I was out here."

"How would she know that if you were supposed to be incognito?"

"I was man. I was discreet as hell. All I did was sit in the car. I never went anywhere unless I had to pee. Then I went to the bushes."

"Man, you could have got a bottle to pee in or something. I just needed you to watch her for two days, dude. That's it and you couldn't even handle that."

"I'm sorry, Man."

"All right, just sit tight. I'll try to call her to see where she is. Don't go anywhere until I call you back."

"I got you, Man and I'm sorry," said the male caller before he hung up.

"Hey, I brought you some juice to go with your sandwich," Kimberly said as she came down the stairs with a plate and a glass. "It's pineapple juice."

"Thank you," Carl said, placing his phone face down on the couch.

"I heard you down here on the phone. Is everything okay?" She asked.

"Yeah, that was just my boy, Tim. He was just checking in to see if I wanted to hang out tonight. I told him that I would call back later," Carl said, using this as a chance to make a phone call later.

"Oh, how is Tim? I haven't heard you talk about him in a long time."

"Tim is still Tim," Carl laughed.

"Is he still with that crazy girl. What's her name, Connie?"

"Oh no, Connie was like five women ago. He's long moved on."

"Oh wow," Kim said as she walked back up the stairs.

Carl grabbed his phone and searched the contacts for the name Tonya. When he found it, he hit the call button. He placed the phone to his ear and waited. The phone on the other end didn't ring and went straight to the automated standard voicemail message.

Carl hung up the phone and sent a text.

Tee, where are you? I just want to make sure that you're okay.

He waited for a response, but none came. He began to get nervous. Where could she be? He didn't want to think that she was where he thought she might be. He needed to know what she was doing. He hoped that she didn't get impatient. He just needed her to wait a few more hours until he completed this grand opening. Once this thing was over, things would be whatever she needed them to be.

Please call me when you get this text, he wrote and placed his phone on vibrate. He didn't want his phone to ring with Kimberly in the room.

Kimberly came back down the stairs with another plate and a glass of juice.

"What you watching?" She asked, looking at the television.

"Oh, something on sports center. I'm not really watching it."

"Okay. So, time is winding down. We are down to the last hour."

"Yeah, it's almost here. Life as we know it, will be gone. Hopefully, to something better and more exciting."

"Yeah, hopefully," Kim repeated. "Do you really believe that this is the way, Carl?"

"I don't know if this is the way, but I believe that it is a way."

"What if it doesn't work? What if it only makes things worse? What do we do then?"

"I don't know; I guess we will just have to cross that bridge when we get to it."

"This might be the end of us, Carl. Doesn't that disturb you in any way?"

"No, because I'm not thinking negatively about it. Look, we just had a good time. Let's not ruin it with negative thoughts."

"Okay, if you say so."

Carl sat quietly eating his sandwich and looking at the television. He knew that the outcome of their grand opening wasn't going to be what Kimberly hoped. It was his intention to ensure that it was not. He needed Kimberly to feel bad about it all once it was done. He needed to be able to blame the whole thing on her, which would give him a solid foundation to make any decisions afterward. Though, he was not sure what any of those decisions would be.

"Kim?" he said.

"Yeah," she answered.

Carl paused, "Never mind."

"Is everything okay, Carl?"

"Yeah, it's good."

Carl was not sure what he was about to say to her, but he felt like he needed to say something. There were way too many awkward moments between them in the past hour and he just wanted to find the words that would make the entire situation more comfortable. It seemed that the sex that they had just had should have done the trick, but it only succeeded in making the tension so thick that you could cut it with a butter knife. It rekindled something in him that almost made him feel guilty for the plan and thoughts that he would put into motion in just a few minutes.

"I do love you, Kim," he said.

"For some reason, Carl, I believe you. I don't feel like I should but, I really do."

"That's good to know."

"The problem is that I'm starting to wonder if love is enough. There was a time when I believed that love was all you needed and that it could conquer any and everything. Now I'm not so sure."

"Sometimes, you just got to trust your heart."

"My heart is what gets me into most of the mess that I find myself in. My head tries to talk me out of it, but I don't know how not to follow my heart. I guess that's a problem that I have."

"Kim, I know you probably don't believe that I see it this way, but your heart will never steer you wrong. Always follow it. It knows best. That's what I try to do. The problem is most people can't tell their head from their heart most of the time."

"They think they are following their heart, but it's the fear in their heads that's guiding them. Fear is never in the heart. Fear only exists to kill the heart. It's the ultimate heart breaker. Always follow your heart, Kim."

"You're right. I am surprised to hear you say that. It seems that you don't want me to follow my heart. You are my heart and I want to keep you."

"I hear Kim and I believe you. But my head is saying different. In this case, I don't know how to follow my heart. My heart is in a bad place right now. It's not in a position to lead me."

"That makes no sense, Carl but I'll leave it alone. You can't give me that speech that you just sprouted off and then make yourself exempt from your own advice."

"I know it sounds hypocritical and maybe it will all become clear for both of us in the next few hours." At least that what he was hoping. He was hoping that it would all become clear, and he could push his total plan into fruition.

PART THREE

TARA MONTGOMERY

8 SECRETS AND LIES

"Where are you?"

"At my mother's house."

"Did anyone see you leave?"

"I don't think so, but I know that the guy sitting outside my house didn't see. I waited for him to go in the bushes and then I went out the back window."

"Nice. So how long can you stay where you are? Can you stay overnight?"

"Yeah, my mother loves when I stay over. She's always talking about how we don't spend enough time together."

"Okay, good. That's what I need. I need him to be in panic mode."

"Well, this will definitely do it. He's been blowing up my phone for the past twenty minutes, so I'm assuming that his little friend told him I was gone. It took him long enough to figure it out," Tonya laughed.

"That's what they get for trying to be gangster," Kimberly said.

"You know, girl."

"Well, sit tight and I'll call you later tonight so we can figure out what's next."

"Okay, I'll talk to you later. I love you."

"I love you too. Bye, bye."

"Bye."

Kimberly ended the phone call and smiled to herself. She was beginning to feel comfortable that this whole thing might work out. She was a bit in doubt when she woke up this morning, but as this day progresses, she's becoming a bit more confident. She wanted to give Carl the benefit of the doubt and an opportunity to undo all of this, but she realized that there was no chance of it. Once she realized this, she knew that she had to find another way. It surprised her that this was going so well since she had just come up with this on the last day.

She flushed the toilet and turned on the bathroom fan for good measure and to give Carl the impression that she had a good reason to have been in the bathroom for as long as she was in there. She fixed her clothes and walked back to where he was sitting.

"Are you okay," he asked.

"Yeah, I guess the mayonnaise on that sandwich is messing with my stomach."

"That's just why I don't eat that stuff."

"Yeah, maybe I should consider giving it up too."

"I keep telling you."

"I know."

"This is the wrong time for your stomach to be messed up. You don't want your stomach to be bubbling when you should be thinking about other things," Carl laughed as he nudged her shoulder.

"Shut up, nasty," she laughed with him.

"I'm just saying," he said.

"So, what about you?"

"What about me?"

"Are you going to be able to do the do after what we just did? I mean I had you pretty riled up."

"I'll be all right. I'm a big boy. I can handle mine. How about you? I know you don't like the be touched after you get a good one."

"I'm okay and even if I'm not. I'm good at faking. Most men don't know the difference anyway."

"Wait a minute, what are you trying to say?"

"I'm not trying to say anything. I just know that even if I'm not feeling it, he won't know the difference," Kim laughed.

"That's messed up. You've been faking with me?"

"Oh no baby, of course not."

"Kim, stop playing. Have you ever faked it with me?"

"No, I haven't."

"Would you tell me if you did?"
"I don't know. Probably not."
"Why not? I can handle it. You can tell me the truth."
"I am telling you the truth. I have never faked with you, Carl," she lied.

Kimberly had not only faked orgasms, but she had also faked enjoyment. There were times when her mind was not in a place for sex, but he insisted on doing it so, she had to do what it took to help him finish quicker. Not to mention, she always saw it as her wifely duty to make sure her man got what he needed, when he needed. Even if that meant having sex when she really didn't feel like it, she had made it a point in her marriage to never say no and when she did, she would always ask for a rain check. When she got a rain check for him to do it later, she always made sure the deed was completed within twelve hours of when she made the promise.

"Okay, I believe you. But you know that's messed up. You have a lot of brothers running around here disillusioned about how good they are in bed because all of you women are lying."

"That's not my problem. Y'all should be confident in your skills; then it won't make a difference if she lies or not. Or she won't need to fake."

"Well, you do need confirmation sometimes.

I mean, I don't need it, but it does help."

"Self-esteem baby. That's all it takes. Isn't that what men talk about all the time? They want women to have self-worth and not need validation from their men. That goes both ways."

"This is different. Every man wants to believe that he is the Adonis for his woman and that she wants no other man but him. He needs to be her everything when it comes to sex. His goal is always to put it on her so good that she will forget that there are other men on the planet. She needs to forget every other man that she's ever been with. It needs to be so good for her that she starts looking for him in the daytime with a flashlight?"

"Oh my God," Kimberly laughed out loud. "In the daytime with a flashlight? I don't think no one has had it that good. At least not any women that I know."

"Well, then you have been with the wrong men."

"Including you?"

"I know that I've put it on you. Hell, I just did it a few minutes ago. You could barely walk when you ran up those stairs."

"Whatever, dude."

"I saw you trying to hurry up and get out of here. You didn't want me to see how weak your knees were," he laughed.

"Yeah, that's what it was. I didn't want you to get a big head, but I see it didn't work."

"Nope and it never will. I am the man and will always be."

"Okay, if you say so."

"You don't think I'm the man?"

"You aight."

"You crazy, I'm better than aight. I'm the man and you're the man the last time I checked."

"Yes, you are my man, which means I have to accept you for what you are no matter what."

"So, what you trying to say."

"Nothing. I'm not trying to say anything. It's my responsibility to help my man believe in himself."

"I do believe in myself and nothing you can say would make me feel less."

"That's good because I would never try to knock you down. I told you it's my role to build you up," she laughed again.

"Okay, I'm quitting before you start messing with my ego," he laughed. "Have me second-guessing myself."

"No, you don't need to do that. I might not be looking for you in the daytime with a flashlight but, I will admit that I am always paying attention to where you are."

"Now that's what I'm talking about. I'm the man."

"Yes, you're the man. You got it."
"Thank you."

Kimberly was doing whatever it took to keep this conversation going. She needed him to continue to think that he had the upper hand in this situation and that she needed him unconditionally. It was becoming harder for her to continue with the line of thinking that she could not make it without him. When she woke up this morning, she had to put herself into the mind frame that their marriage could survive if he only believed that she loves him unconditionally and if he knew that she would do anything for him. It seems that this approach was not working for him, so she has decided to change her position. She figured if she pushed his ego, he would become so cocky that he would screw up his own plan and make hers work perfectly.

"So what time is it? How much more time before they get here?" She asked.

"Just under an hour now," Carl said, looking at his watch.

"You excited?"

"A little bit. How about you?"

"Not excited. Nervous."

"Why?"

"This is a lot. I don't know if I can do this. It was hard for me to cheat on you, whether you want to believe it or not, Carl."

"Well, the good thing is this is not cheating. I know what's going on. That should take off a lot of the pressure. I know it does for me."

"Yes, but I dedicated my life to you and now I'm going against my own promise. I'm someone that believes in what I say, and I stick to something when I say it."

"Well, in this case, it's all good. Don't be nervous. I got your back."

"How? How do you have my back?"

"I'm in this with you. We are doing this together."

"That doesn't really help, and it doesn't feel like we are in this together. It feels like it's the beginning of the end."

"The beginning of the end of what?"

"Of us. I don't see how we will have any relationship after this," Kimberly said, warning him without warning him.

"I don't see why you think we won't. Sex is not at the root of our relationship. We don't even have sex that much, Kim."

"Yes, but we are a team, and this is almost like adding new players to the team or should I say adding new slots to the roster. It used to be a roster of two players and now we are adding two more slots to be filled by anyone that wants to play."

"Well, if you want to be honest, it looks like the new slots were always on the team, but we never wanted to admit that we were filling them to one another. Now, at least we are being honest about it."

"I guess. Well, I'm still nervous just the same."

"It's going to be okay, Kim. If you want, I'll talk to the dude before we start, just so everyone can get a warm and fuzzy. How about that?"

"Assuming that you aren't already involved with your friend when he gets here."

"We'll wait until everyone is here, okay?"

Carl had said exactly what she wanted to hear. She needed him to be present when both parties arrived at their home.

"Really? Okay, I like that idea. I think that will help. Thank you."

"I told you I got you."

Kimberly sat quiet, thinking about their conversation. She tried to imagine what the meeting would be like when everyone was in the same room. It was going to be a site to see and a lot to handle. She knew that it would take a lot to get through it and that the real emotions would happen when it was time for all the mess to hit the fan. She just had to make sure that she came out on top of this situation and that Carl got just what he deserved.

"So have you still not decided where you want to do it yet?" He asked.

"Would it bother you if I used the bedroom?"

"I'm not sure. I think it would bother me. I don't know if I would be able to sleep there ever again. Not to mention have sex with you in that bed."

"So, we were planning to still have sex with one another after this too?"

"Yes, who said we were done having sex?"

"I just assumed that since you were having such a problem forgiving from the cheating that you wouldn't want to be with me like that after today."

"How could you assume that after what we just did?"

"I don't know. I guess I just assumed that you distanced yourself and it was almost like the final countdown."

"No Kim. I love having sex with you. I love the way you, well you know. I enjoy what we have."

"Okay, so I guess the bedroom is off-limits."

"Yes, thank you. It's like a sanctuary. Not to mention, we already said that we couldn't do it in the house at all after today."

"Yeah, I remember."

"You know you can use the spare bedroom down here in the basement?"

"I thought that you were using that room."

"I can use this couch right here. I'm not

going to be long. It will be over before you know it. I just want to give it to shorty. This is not about her. It's about you and me. Those two coming over here are just pawns in our plans. They mean nothing. Well, at least that's how I'm looking at it."

"I see it the same way. I just didn't want to assume that you would be looking it like that too. But I do need to be comfortable. I'm not going to just let him manhandle me."

"I feel you," Carl said as he put his head down.

Kimberly noticed that it seemed that this conversation was beginning to wear down on him. Was he having a change of heart? Was he growing a conscious? Was her change in attitude and approach beginning to affect him? If it was, it was too late. She was not going to back out of this. He deserved whatever came of this. He started it and she was going to finish it. He had hurt her one time too many and he would never get the opportunity to do it ever again.

"So, it's settled, I'll use the spare bedroom down here and you will use this area. How will we know when it's safe to come back out here. We have to pass here for him to leave."

"We should be done long before you are, but just call out the door to make sure the coast is clear before you step out."

"Okay, I can do that."

"Cool."

"You know they are going to think we're crazy and that we are a couple of swingers. They might not be cool with knowing what's going on here."

"My friend already knows what's going on. She knows that you're going to be here and that you are cool with it. You didn't tell your friend?"

"Well, kind of. He knows he's coming to my house, and he knows that you're okay with me messing around, but I don't know if he's expecting you to be here," Kimberly lied.

"Well, he should be okay and if he isn't I'll make sure he knows that it's all good. I'll say whatever it takes to make sure he's all right."

"Sounds good."

"Man, I can't believe that we are actually going to do this."

"Me either. Most people would think that we're crazy."

"Which is why people don't need to know. What we do is our business. Plus, I don't need people trying to get up in your head, making you have second thoughts."

"You know I'm a big girl right and that I make my own decisions."

"I know but sometimes it's easy to be influenced by others, especially when we believe that we aren't thinking clearly."

"Well, I know exactly what I've agreed to. Like you said earlier, this was my own idea, remember?"

"True. And if you're good, then I'm good. I still don't think no one needs to know," Carl said.

"I agree, but do you think that these two will be able to keep it to themselves after this is all said and done."

"Well, the person coming to see me doesn't really associate with anyone that I know. How about you? Do you guys share any mutual friends that he can talk to?"

"No, we don't, plus he's married, and he won't want his wife to find out."

"Kim, you little devil. Look at you, burning the candle at both ends."

"Well, I just figured I needed to get someone who had just as much to lose as I did. I couldn't bring a single person in here. Plus, I didn't want to risk him wanting to get too involved with me."

"Smart thinking. I get it."

"You did do the same thing, right?" Kim asked, already knowing the answer to her question.

"Well, not exactly. I figured she knew that I was married, so she understands that she can only have me on a physical level."

"I don't know if that's good, Carl. Women tend to get emotionally involved very quickly."

"I feel you, but she knows that I'm not leaving my wife."

Another lie that Kimberly recognized.

"Well, so do you believe that she would tell someone?"

"Not if she wants to see me again. I'll make sure that she doesn't. And like I said, we don't share any mutual friends."

"You know that women can be very vindictive, so you better make sure to stay on her good side," Kimberly warned him again.

"She'll be good. I'm not worried about it. I got this," he boasted.

"All right, Carl. I hope you do. I hope you do."

9 CLOSE CALL

"Is that the doorbell?" Kimberly asked.

"What? I didn't hear anything," Carl responded.

"I think I heard the doorbell," Kimberly said, heading toward the basement stairs.

"Who would be ringing the doorbell? It's too early for them to be here. They still have about forty-five minutes," Carl said, looking at his watch as he followed her up the stairs.

The doorbell rang again as they reached the main floor landing.

"I guess someone's early," Carl said.

"Anxious," Kimberly laughed. She walked ahead of Carl to the door and turned on the porch light to see who was on the other side.

"Who is it?" Carl asked, opening the door.

"It's me, Daddy," said a cute little girl with pigtails.

"And me too," said a smaller boy.

Carl smiled at his children as they pushed passed him and ran up the stairs.

Carl looked at his children in astonishment and then back out the door at the woman who was with them.

"Cindy, what are you doing here? Is everything okay," Kimberly asked.

"No, I just had a big fall out with my mother, so we can't stay at her house tonight. I'm sorry. I wish I had somewhere else to take them, but you know I have been staying with my mother since I got laid off from my job."

"Oh, I'm sorry to hear that, Cindy. It's okay."

"No, I know it's not okay. I know you two had plans for this tonight."

"Don't worry about it, girl. We can change our plans. Do it another night."

"Wait a minute. No, we can't change our plans. Slow down. We need to figure this out," Carl said.

"Carl, you heard her. She can't watch the kids tonight. What do you want her to do?"

"I don't know, Kim, but we need to get this worked out."

"There's nothing to get worked out. She can't do it. We can just do this another night."

"We can't do this another night. It has to be tonight. Too much planning went into this. We might not be able to do it another night. This might be a once in a lifetime opportunity."

"Really, Carl. Calm down. It is not that

serious."

"Yes, it is that serious."

"Look, I know you really wanted to do this, and I promise that we will make it happen. Don't worry; I am not going to change my mind. Plus, you know I don't really like to leave the kids with anyone other than Cindy and our parents."

"Kim, let me talk to you in private for a minute," he said, motioning her to walk with him to the kitchen.

"Cindy girl. I'm sorry that you are having problems at home. Please forgive my inconsiderate husband for his crazy behavior. Thank you for bringing the kids home. If you give me a minute, I'll get your money so you can be on your way."

"Okay, I'll just wait right here, and I really am sorry, Kim."

"Stop apologizing; it's not your fault."

Carl walked into the kitchen and waited for Kimberly to arrive. After a few moments, she walked through the door.

"Carl, what is the matter with you? Was all of that really necessary?"

"Look Kim; we've been planning this for too long to call it off now. Plus, they are probably already on their way. We can stop them now."

"Carl, we can just tell them when they get

here. This is not a big deal. We can't do it tonight."

"Kim, I don't care what you say; we are going to figure this out. If Cindy can't watch them, then we can take them to your mother's house."

"My parents are not home, remember? My mother took my father to the Bahamas to celebrate his retirement."

"Okay, then Cindy can take the kids to your mother's house?"

"What? What did you just say? She can do what? Do you really want to have sex with another woman that bad?"

"Forget it. Forget what I just said. I was just brainstorming."

"You damn right we're going to forget it. I'm not going to be just coming up with these last-minute random solutions just because you got a hard on."

"Okay, so I'm going to ignore that last statement, but I am going to figure this out. I'll be right back. I got some phone calls to make."

Carl left the kitchen and headed back out to the living room where Cindy was waiting. He looked back over his shoulder to ensure that Kimberly was not within earshot.

"What the hell is going on? What are you doing here?" He asked.

"I told you what I'm doing here?"

"I thought you said your niece was going to watch them so you could come here."

"She was until my mother found out."

"What do you mean?"

"She heard that I was going out and that I was going to leave the kid with my niece, and she went off. She said if I told someone that I would babysit for them, I should be the one to sit with the kids. She said that I couldn't leave the kids at the house with Jasmin. So, I brought them back early so you could have time to find someone else."

"Oh gee, thanks for nothing. And tell me, how were you going to get back in here. Were you just planning to stay until it was time to start?"

"No, I was going to leave and come back so we could still have the element of surprise."

"Wow, you never cease to amaze me. I'm so glad that you had that figured out," Carl said sarcastically.

"Okay, here you go, Cindy," Kimberly said, reentering the room. "I hope you can work things out with your mother. I know how it is to be living in someone else's house and to be on bad terms with them."

"Girl, it's all right. It's just my momma. She'll get over it. We fight all the time. She just hates it when I don't do the right thing. And you know, she's right. I'm just sorry that I had your kids all up in the middle of it. But they were happy to be coming home."

"I'll be back. I got some phone calls to make," Carl said, leaving the room. "I'll check on the kids while I'm upstairs.

"Okay," Kim responded.

Carl walked up the stairs and to his and Kim's bedroom. He removed his phone from his pocket, found Tony's number, and called it. Tony answered on the first ring.

"Yo, what's up," Tony said.

"Did she come back yet?"

"Nah, man. What you want me to do?"

"Shit," Carl said. "Just stay there; I'm going to try to call her again. I'll call you back in a few minutes. I might need you to make a trip for me."

"Okay, man, I'm standing by."

Carl ended the call and then dialed his mother's number. After two rings, she answered.

"Mom, I need your help."

"Is everything all right, Carl."

"Yes, everything's fine. I just need you to let the kids stay at your house tonight."

"Carl, you know I can't do that. I can't watch them and watch your father at the same time. We already had this conversation."

"It won't be for the whole night. It will only be for a couple of hours. I promise."

"What's going on? Where's Kim," his mother asked.

"Nothing is going on and Kim is right here. We just made plans and our babysitter just fell through. We had reservations at a restaurant and hotel and now we are going to lose money because it's too late to cancel either," he lied.

"Carl, I'm sorry, but I just can't do it. I have to make sure that your father gets his meds every two hours, and I can't watch him and those kids at the same time. You know how busy they get."

"Ma, you know I wouldn't ask you this if I had any other option. Please help me. I will owe you big time after this."

"I don't want you to owe me, and you won't because I told you that I can't do it."

"Ma, please."

"No, and get off my phone," his mother said as she ended the call without saying goodbye.

"Damn," Carl said, staring at the phone. He tried to think of who else he could call. He could think of no one else, especially not anyone that Kim would approve of. This was a bad situation. He needed to make this happen. He had too many things at stake. He needed to get to Tonya before it was too late, and she had the abortion. He needed Kim to get mad enough to break up with him, so he could go start his life with Tonya, but if she had the abortion, she would never have him. She would only blame him for making her get rid of yet another baby. He could not have that happen. Tonya was the only woman that he ever truly loved. He had almost lost her once and he was not going to let that happen again. No, he had to find some way to figure this whole situation out. He had to find someone to keep the kids so; this thing grand opening of his marriage fiasco could go down tonight.

He walked down the hall to his daughter's room where both children were playing.

"Hey crazies, what are you guys doing?"

"Playing," they answered in unison."

"Really, what are you playing?" Carl asked.

"Horses," the kids said together again.

"Oh, how fun," he said.

"You want to play with us, Daddy," the little girl asked.

"Of course, but I have to go back downstairs and make sure Mommy's all right first. I'll come back right after."

"Okay, Daddy," she said as she continued to play with her horse, seeming to instantly forget about her father.

Carl got up and left the room. He walked back down the stairs to where the two women still sat talking.

"So, Cindy, if I give you money for a hotel room, would you take the kids with you tonight?"

"Carl," Kimberly barked. "Have you lost your ever-loving mind?"

"No, I haven't. I told you this is going down. Well, would you?"

Cindy looked at Kimberly. Her mouth moved as she shook her head, but no words came out.

"Don't answer that, Cindy," Kimberly said. "Carl stop it."

"You stop it, Kim. Well, would you, Cindy?" Carl asked again, trying to give her a look that told her to say that she would.

Cindy hesitated as she moved her eyes back and forth between the two people. Both seemed to will her to say yes. After a few moments, she shook her head up and down.

"Sure, I guess," she said skeptically.

"Great, then it's solved," Carl said, digging into his pocket.

"No, it's not, Kim said. "Are you kidding me."

"No, I'm not. Be quiet, Kim. I got this and it's solved. Cindy here's two hundred dollars."

"Carl,"

"Quit, Kim. Cindy that should be more than enough for a room for one night. If you need more, just call me from the hotel and tell me what you need."

"Okay," Cindy said, taking the money from

his hand. "I'll go upstairs and get the kids ready."

"You do that," Carl said.

He looked at Kim, who was shaking her head. He walked through the kitchen and back to the basement door. When he arrived, he called Tony again.

"Did she come back?" He asked once Tony answered.

"Come one man, you know she's still gone."

"Okay, I need you to ride past Planned Parenthood and see if you see her car."

"What?" Tony asked. "You need me to do what?"

"I just need you to do a drive-by and see if you see her, that's all."

"Dude, I'm not going to that crazy place. Plus, her car is still out here. She didn't take her car."

"What? She left and she didn't drive?"

"Yeah, I'm telling you her car is still here."

"Are you sure she's not in the house?"

"There's no lights on and it's dark out here."

"That don't mean anything, man. She could still be in there."

"I doubt it. I haven't seen any movement."

"Yo, you need to check. Maybe she never left. She might still be in there."

"Dude, I told you nobody's home. Plus, you know I can't go over there and ring the doorbell."

"Well, find somebody else to do it."

"Seriously, dude."

"Yeah, man."

"Look, Son, she's not in there. Take my word for it."

"All right man. I believe you. I'm tripping. I know it. I just don't want this to fall through and it's already on the path."

"Man, she told you that she was going to keep the baby, right?"

"Yeah, but only after I told her that I was going to leave Kim, so we can be a family."

"So, don't worry about it. You just have to make it through tonight and trust that she is going to do what she said. I mean, has she ever lied to you?"

"No, she hasn't but I've lied enough to her for the both of us. I don't know if she trusts me enough to wait for me."

"She's been waiting for you all this time, right?"

"Yeah, man."

"Then this shouldn't be any different," Tony said.

"Well, if that's the case, then where is she?" Carl asked.

"Now, that I don't know but, if she's like most other women, she's only trying to make you nervous right now and I would say that it's working."

"Yeah, man. You might be right."

"I am right, so you need to stop fretting and calm down."

"I still wish I knew where she was," Carl said.

"I know. Look I'm going to sit out here for the rest of the night like we planned. I'll hit you up if and when she comes back."

"All right man. Talk to you later."

"Hey, keep your head up and do what you got to do on your part. You don't want the whole plan to unravel."

"I feel you, dude. Thanks. Later."

"Later," Tony said as he hung up the phone.

As he ended the call, Cindy came down the stairs.

"Okay, well, we're out of here."

"What hotel will you be staying in?" Carl asked.

"I called the Holiday Inn Express. It's only a few miles from here. Makes it easy, so the kids aren't in the car too long. I told them we were going to the hotel and that they had a swimming pool, so it didn't take much to make them want to come with me," Cindy said.

"That was smart thinking," Kimberly said.

"Yeah, way to think on your feet," he said, giving her a knowing look.

"Thanks. Well, we'll get out of your hair,"

Cindy said, pushing the children toward the door.

"Hey wait. Give mommy a kiss," Kim said to the children. She leaned over and planted kisses on both of their heads.

"Bye, Mommy," the little boy said.

"See you later, Sweetie," Kim said.

"Bye Babies," Carl said.

"Bye Daddy," they answered in unison.

"Okay, well, have a good night," Cindy said as the three walked out of the door.

"Okay, Cindy and thanks again," Kimberly said.

"Anytime, girl," Cindy said.

Carl closed the door behind them and returned to the basement.

10 LET THE REAL GAMES BEGIN

Kimberly sat on the couch and stared into the quiet of the room. She was pleased with where the situation had gone. Her plan was going so well, and she could not believe that Carl had not figured out what she was up to yet. He usually is a lot more suspicious. Kimberly assumed that he was so vested in his own little plan that he had not considered that someone would know that he was up to something.

When he left the room while Cindy was still at the house, Kimberly waited until he was out of earshot to talk to her.

"Oh my God, girl. This is so crazy," she said.

"I know, girl. I was so nervous. I was afraid that he would give it all up and agree with you. You were pushing so hard for him to stop."

"I did, but I knew that he wouldn't. He is too vain to be defeated that quickly. He would have never let it go. Girl, he would have given those kids to a stranger on the street first," Kim laughed.

"That is so amazing to me. I can't believe how bad he wanted to keep going. I mean he would not let it go."

"I told you he wouldn't. But I really want to thank you for doing this for me."

"Look, I'm just happy that you believed me when I told you that he has been looking at me funny for years. I knew that he wanted to get with me, and I wanted you to know that I would never do anything like that to you. I value our friendship."

"Well, let me tell you, it wasn't easy for me to believe you. I want my marriage to be perfect like any other woman on the planet. It's hard to hear that your husband is unfaithful, especially when it's being done in your own home," Kim said.

"Well, I tell you, it was hard. I didn't know if I should tell you. I was afraid and I really didn't know how to handle it. I contemplated it for months. But then I knew that I was going to have to tell you if I wanted to keep babysitting for you."

"Well, once again, thank you so much for that and thank you for this. So, now when he comes down, whatever he comes up with, I need you to accept it. I'm going to keep acting like I want him to stop it, but you just say yes and please watch out for my children."

"You know I won't ever let anything happen to those kids. I'm just going to take them back to the house where they were."

"Okay, that's fine. And you said that your niece is going to sit with them when you come back. Yes, don't worry about it. She's great with kids. She teaches at a daycare."

"Girl, I'm not worried. I trust you and you are helping me on this."

"Okay then."

"Just remember that I'm going to act crazy and lose my mind when I see you here again later. It's only an act."

"I know, just don't hit me."

"I promise I won't," Kimberly laughed.

"This is so crazy," Cindy said right before Carl came back down the stairs.

Kimberly sat back on the couch. She closed her eyes and took a deep breath. She needed to get her mind together and get herself ready for the show that she was about to put on at their little rendezvous. Carl was not going to know what hit him. He was about to get everything that he deserved and dished out to her over the past few years. Kimberly knew that she was going to have to keep her nerve up and not chicken out of her plan. She still loved Carl and it was going to be hard to see him go through this thing that she was planning for him. She didn't want her feeling to get involved and change her mind. She knew that she had to remain strong and go through all the way to the end. This was going to take a lot of guts.

She stood up from the couch and headed downstairs to the basement where Carl was shooting pool again.

"Carl, what was that? What is going on with you, she asked?"

"Nothing is going on with me. We just have something to do, and I was making sure that it happens without a glitch."

"At the expense of the safety of your children, Carl?"

Hell no. My kids were not in any danger. She was just having a problem at her house, but she didn't have a problem keeping the kids. So, I fixed her house problem. Stop worrying. It all worked out in the end and now we are back on track for the grand opening. All is well."

"All is well? Is that all you got?" Kimberly asked.

"What more do you want, Kim. I mean I worked hard to make sure that we got to where we are, and I am not going to let my hard work go to waste."

"What hard work are you referring to? I mean, all I had to do was make a few phone calls."

"That's all that I had to do too. I was just saying I had to work at getting the girl that I got for this. That's all I meant."

Kimberly almost had to laugh at his blunder. He almost blew his whole situation.

"I should have known it had something to do with sex. You are never going to change."

"What's the big deal? Isn't that what we planned to do?
You should have been helping me ensure that this thing still went down. Except you were ready to throw the towel in at the first sign of trouble."

"Carl, there was no trouble. We had no one to watch our children. There is no way I'm going to just send my kids out anywhere simply so you can have sex with some whore."

"Last time I checked, you were about to do the same thing and you didn't stop me when push came to shove. That's all I'm saying."

"Because you were so adamant about making sure it happened and sending her to a hotel. I mean, you gave her two hundred dollars for one night. Where did you think she was going to stay, at the Waldorf Astoria?"

"Well, it's a hotel and the kids have to eat. So, she's going to need money for that. It's not like she can cook something."

"Whatever, I hear you. I'm going to let it go, the same way I did earlier."

"Of course, you are. You want this just as bad as I do. You just don't want to admit it."

Of all the things that Carl had said to her today, this was the one thing that she really did agree with. He was one hundred percent correct. Kimberly did want this to happen just as bad as he did. She needed to see this to the end. She had to see the look on his face when he realized that she was planning to leave him and the marriage. She was fed up with being hurt by him and was intent on teaching him a lesson. Yes, he was correct in saying that she wanted it just as bad.

"You're right, Carl. I would like to see this day come to fruition. And it's all going to be going down in the next thirty minutes."

"It's been a long two hours, I'll tell you. I'll actually be happy when it's all said and done. Today has been one big roller coaster ride and I think I'm just about ready to get off."

"Literally," Kimberly laughed.

"Touché," Carl joined her.

"But you know you just got off a little while ago."

"Yeah, I did, and now I'm just about ready for round two."

"You are so nasty."

"That's not nasty. It's the truth. I'm a man. You never get too much. The goal is always to get as much as you can."

"Of course, it is. Never had a doubt."

"You know your female mind will never

understand the needs of a man, right?" Carl asked.

"Needs. These are not needs, they are wants and they are guided by greed and lust."

"Call it what you want, but it's still a man thing that you will never fully comprehend."

"You know part me is very happy about that. If I start understanding men, I don't think I would recognize myself. Not to mention, I don't want to be in the know about anything male. I'm totally happy and content being the woman that I am."

"That's fine with me. Just don't hate on the way we see the world. You'll never get it figured out, so just let it be."

"Let it be, huh? Ok whatever you say, Sir,"

"Thank you very much. You do that and I won't try to figure out how any of you crazy women think."

"Why do we have to be crazy?"

"Because all of you are. You have the craziest way of seeing the world. Women make things so much more difficult than they need to be."

"No, we simplify everything. The problem is that we dumb it down so far that you guys can't keep up. You think it's far more sophisticated than it is, and you get lost in the shuffle."

"Look at you using big words, lost in the shuffle. That's so cute," Carl joked.

"Whatever. You will never understand the mind of a woman because your meager thought patterns can't measure up."

"You know you're right," Carl said, walking away from the pool table and over to the bar. He poured himself a glass of water and drank it straight down. Kimberly walked over to where he stood. "I would never try to jump into a woman's mind. I'm afraid I might get lost in there and never be able to return. Help I'm in the twilight zone."

"You are so stupid," Kim laughed. "I don't know why I even waste my time talking to you."

"Because you know that I'm highly intelligent and you like to hear my views on these types of topics."

"You're right. I love using you as comic relief. It makes my day so much more interesting. The sad part is that you really believe that you are bestowing some kind of knowledge on me."

"I am, especially with this whole grand opening thing. You might be taking it too seriously. It's all about being loose and freeing yourself. Being content in who you are and in the situation."

"Say what you want, Carl, but this is something different and it's not that easy to just be taking lightly. You deal with it your way and I'll handle it my own way."

"I feel you and excuse me for having an opinion. I won't say anything else. I'll just sit here quiet for the next thirty minutes and wait for your friend to arrive, so I can see how corny he is," Carl laughed.

"Corny. I don't mess with corny men."

"He has to be corny because he's not me. Any dude that you mess with after me will never live up to what and who I am."

"You really believe that this world, I mean, my world revolves around you."

"Isn't that what you said earlier?"

"I said I love you and would choose not to share my husband, but I didn't say that you were the center of the universe. There's only one being in my center and that would be the Lord above. Don't get it twisted. You are definitely in second place when it comes to him."

"Well, last time I checked, the Lord told women to honor and obey their husbands."

"True, but he didn't say put them on a pedestal. Like I said, I love you, but you are not all that makes me who I am. I think that together we make a great team. I believe that this has the potential to change that but, if you're confident that it won't, then I'll follow your lead, husband."

"Oh, so now I'm a husband."

"You've always been. I just don't think that

you know it and if you do, you don't know what it means."

"Oh wow, that's low."

"I'm sorry. I just call it how I see it. But what do you care. You're about to have someone come over and make it all better for you. Isn't that great?"

"Be quiet, girl. I'm done talking to you. I'm going to just take a quick nap for the next few minutes until they get here."

"Ok, fine. I'm done talking. I'll leave you be."

Kimberly stood up and walked back up the stairs. It was a good idea for him to want to take a nap. It gave her the time that she needed just to get her mind right. She walked up the second flight of stairs and to her bedroom, closing the door behind her. She turned the lamp on and sat on the bed. She couldn't believe that in just a few minutes, she would no longer consider herself a married woman. She also would be from under the heaviness that has become her marriage. She would emerge a new person with a lot less concerns. Her mind will be free to consider all of the possibilities of a new life. She lay back on the bed and imagined her new self.

After a few minutes, she sat back up and pulled her cell phone from her pocket. She located Tonya's number in her contacts and hit the call button. Tonya answered after the second ring.

"Hello," Tonya said.

"Hey, I was just calling to make sure we are still good."

"Yeah, I'm still coming."

"I thought that you said you left your car, so how are you going to get here?"

"Oh, I'm going to use my mother's car. Which is good because he won't recognize the car when I get there."

"Yes, that's right. That's great thinking."

"So, what's up with you? You okay? You sound a bit stressed."

"I'm a little nervous about all of this and Carl has been driving me crazy all day. I didn't relax until we. I mean until I was able to walk away."

"Until you what?"

"Oh nothing, I wasn't going to say anything."

"Yes, you were, Kim. You were going to say something. What was it?"

"Nothing. I wasn't about to say anything."

"Kim, stop playing with me. I know you, now what was it?"

"I don't know what you're talking about."

"Did you have sex with Kim?"

"No, I didn't."

"Kim, stop lying to me. You did something with him, didn't you? That's why you sound stressed. You were calling to tell me, weren't you? That's why you wanted to know if I was okay, right?"

"Tonya, I'm sorry. I didn't mean to. It just happened."

"Really Kim, you just slipped and fell on top of him?"

"Well, I mean, he is my husband. I can have sex with my husband."

"Seriously? You're joking right? Kim, we had a pact. Neither one of us would sleep with him again. We would not let ourselves get sucked in. Come on now."

"Okay, I'm sorry. You're right."

"I don't want to be right. I just want to make sure this thing comes off without a hitch. You can't be weak up there. I need to know that you are going to see the plan through to the end."

"I will. I'm not going to mess this up. We need this for the both of us."

"How do you know you haven't already messed it up. He hasn't called me. So maybe he's not worried about me getting rid of the baby anymore, after your little episode."

"First of all, you mean imaginary baby and no he hasn't changed his mind. Believe me. If anything, he's gotten more into the idea."

"For your sake, I hope you're right."

"For our sake. We are going to do this together. We already said that."

"We were but you seem to be changing the rules."

"I said I'm sorry. I had a moment of weakness. It won't happen again."

"All right. Please don't let it happen again."

"I won't, but there's not enough time left for me to do anything wrong anyway. We have less than thirty minutes before you guys are supposed to be here."

"Did you speak to Cindy?"

"Yes, she just left here. He sent her to a hotel with the kids."

"A hotel? You're kidding me."

"No, I'm not. He would not let it go. I tried and no matter how hard I pushed; he would not let it go. You should have seen him. He was in total panic mode. You got him. He is so worried about being with you and that baby that he couldn't think straight. As mad as it makes me because he had no concern for our kids. It was pathetic, actually."

"I'm sorry, Kim. I really am. I didn't mean for this to hurt you or the kids."

"I know, Tonya and believe it or not, I don't blame you. I just wish you had told me a long time ago. Maybe you could have saved me a few years of hurt."

"You're right, I should have told you. I owed you that. I can't apologize enough, but that's why we have to make sure that this goes off without a hitch. He needs to get what he deserves."

"He will, if it's the last thing I do.

"I need to make sure to give Cindy enough time to get there and to give you enough time to freak out about it."

"You want me to text you when she gets here? That way, you know when to come."

"No, you can't text me because you're supposed to be freaking out. I'll hit up Cindy and tell her to text me before she goes in the house."

"Okay, give it about ten minutes before you leave the house, after she contacts you. I'm going to need time to make a big deal about the whole thing."

"I feel you. This is going to be so fun. I can't wait until he sees me and to see the look on his face. This is going to be priceless. Oh my God."

"I know right. This is going to be priceless."

"Priceless and unforgettable. I am never going to stop reliving this day."

"I just hope that I don't feel bad later. I don't want to regret leaving him the next day."

"See, I knew the sex was a bad idea. You are getting weak already."

"No, I'm not. I got it. I'm okay,"

"Look Kim, don't mess this up. We have too much riding on all of this. We are all going to finally be able to move on with our lives. The past won't have a hold on us anymore."

"Tonya, I'm good. I promise. Don't worry about me. I got this."

"I hope you do, Kim. This has to happen. Carl has to get what he deserves. He has to get what's coming to him."

"He will," Kim said as she ended the call and fell back on the bed. She took a deep breath and closed her

TARA MONTGOMERY

11 MEMORIES AND DECISIONS

Carl pulled the key from the ignition and opened the car door. He stepped out of the car and looked at the brick building across the street. He hesitated a few seconds as he tried to muster the courage to go inside. After a few moments, he walked across the street. As he neared the building, he could hear the chants of the people that were protesting near the front door. A scene like this would normally bother him and make him detour from his plans, but he needed to get inside. He had to get to Tonya before she did anything crazy. He could not let her get rid of his baby. He had made that mistake once before and there was no way he was going to repeat the sins of the past. Back then, he had the opportunity to do the right thing, but he was afraid, so he ran away. Now it was almost twenty years later and here they were in the same predicament. He was not going to make the same mistake twice. He was going to prove to her that he could be a better man than he was back then. He was going to live up to his responsibility and be a father to this child. They were going to be a family if it was the last thing that he ever did.

Carl walked past the picketers and walked into the building. One of the women was trying to get his attention, but he ignored her and continued on his way. Nothing was going to stop him. He walked to the counter and spoke to the receptionist.

"Good morning, Ma'am" he said. "I'm looking for Tonya James."

"Oh, um, are you her husband?"

"Yes," he lied.

"Oh good, she's expecting you," the receptionist said.

"Really?" Carl said, surprised at the nurse's last comment.

"Yes, she said that you might show up. I just need to see your identification to verify who you are."

Carl pulled out his driver's license and handed it to her. The woman looked at it and handed it back to him.

"Okay, I'll buzz you in," she said pointing to the door to his left.

Carl walked toward the door and pulled it open just as the buzzer sounded. The woman came from behind the desk.

"She's down the hall in room six," she said,

pointing down the hall.

"Thank you," Carl said as he walked in the direction of the room.

"Good luck and congratulations," she said to him.

"Congratulations?" Carl thought to himself. Why would she say that. This is an abortion clinic. He dismissed the thought as soon as he thought it.

"Thank you," he called back over his shoulder, not noticing the bouquet of flowers that appeared in his hand. He continued down the hall until he arrived at room six. He tightened the string of the balloon that he was also now carrying so it would make it through the threshold of the door. He knocked and waited for a response.

"Come in," he heard Tonya say through the door. "I'm ready."

Carl turned the doorknob and walked into the room. Tonya was sitting on the far end of the bed with her back to the door.

"Hey baby," he said. I brought you some flowers and a balloon." he said.

"Really? Thank you," she said.

"You're welcome. Anything for you," he replied. "Why are you facing backwards, baby?"

"Oh, I wanted it to be a surprise when you came in."

"Oh, that's sweet. You are always trying to

do things for me. Turn around and let me see."

"Are you sure you want to see?" she asked.

"Come on now, you know I want to see my baby. Turn around, Sweetheart," he said.

"Okay, but I hope you're ready," Tonya said.

"I'm here this time. You know I'm ready," he said.

Tonya swung her legs around to face him and as she did, he noticed that her legs were covered in blood.

"Baby, what's that? What's the matter?"

"Nothing's the matter, baby. You said you wanted to see."

"See what, baby?"

Just as he asked, Tonya held out a bloody mass wrapped in a blanket like a baby."

"Isn't she beautiful?" She asked.

"Oh my God. Tonya, what did you do? Where's the baby?"

"She's right here, baby. Don't you see her?"

"Baby, that's not a baby, it's not a baby?"

"Yes, it is. It's our baby. Isn't this what you wanted? You said you wanted this. Take it," she screamed. "Take it."

"No, I don't want it," Carl cried. "I don't want it."

He opened his eyes and looked around. He was back on the couch in his man cave. He wiped his face. He had been crying in his sleep. He knew that he had been dreaming, but it all felt so real. He couldn't believe that he was having the dream again. He really needed to fix this situation before he lost his mind and the love of his life. He had enough regrets for how he handled that situation so many years ago that he seemed to be losing his mind. This was also the reason that he found it so difficult to commit and stay loyal to Kimberly. He had so much unfinished business with Tonya that he didn't know how to dedicate himself to Kimberly. There was a part of him that felt bad about all the mistreatment that Kimberly had to endure at his expense. Then, in another area, he felt that he was wrong for even marrying her. Carl knew that he could never say this to Kimberly. He could never tell her the truth. He knew that she would be hurt and feel like the last ten years of her life were not real. They were real. He did love Kim. She was the mother of his children, but he felt he owed his life to Tonya. He had taken so much from her, that he felt he had to spend a lifetime trying to give it back to her.

He stood up from the chair as he looked for his cell phone. He needed to speak to Tonya and tell her to hold on. He knew that she wanted to terminate her pregnancy because she did not trust that he would be there for her. He knew that she believed that he didn't want the baby. Tonya was also a woman with morals, and he knew that she would not be able to live with the idea of hurting Kim. It wasn't that the women were friends, but she was Carl's wife and Tonya believed that she deserved a certain amount of respect. Carl thought about how she tried to explain it to him.

"Carl, it's okay. You don't have to worry about it. I'm letting you off the hook," Tonya said.

"No, Baby, I'm going to be here with you this time. We are in this together no matter what."

"Carl, you can't be here. You are a married man. I should not have let us get into this. This is wrong, but I was weak because I've always loved you. I wouldn't be able to live with myself, knowing that I was pulling you away from your wife and children. Children need their dad."

"I agree and that's why I'm trying to tell you that I will be there for you this time. You don't have to do what I think you want to do."

"You mean to get an abortion? I have to, Carl. This is wrong and it's not right for us to subject this baby to a life of dysfunction."

Yes, I don't want you to get an abortion, especially because you think that I don't want to be here for you, Tonya. I'm trying to tell you that not only do I want you. I want our baby too. I'm not mad that you are pregnant. I'm actually excited about it. I get the chance to fix the mess that I made so long ago."

"Carl, you can't fix the past. It's already happened, and it's already gone."

"You're right. I can't fix it, but I can make it up to you. I can prove to you that I'm a better person than that guy from back then. I can show you that I will never abandon you again."

"Carl, you are married. What about your wife? What about Kim?"

"Why don't you let me worry about my wife and my marriage? I can handle this."

"No, Carl, this is wrong, and I can't be a part of it."

"Tonya, I can't make you do this again. I can't take it. I need the dreams to stop."

"Are you still having those dreams?" Tonya asked.

"They stopped for a little while, but now they're back. They came back when you told me that you were pregnant. I think it's whenever I know that I have a baby on the way. The same thing happened when Kim was pregnant with both kids. I know that I should not have done what I did to you. I should have never made you get rid of our baby. I have been living with guilt for so many years. Please give me an opportunity to make it better."

"Carl, you can't make this better for me. You have to make it better for yourself and making it better for yourself has nothing to do with me. You need to start with self-compassion. You need to first forgive yourself. You are so stuck on trying to prove to me that you are worthy of my love, but you have to start by loving yourself. You can't show me that you love me, if you don't have any love inside to give. This is why you have been so unfaithful to your wife."

"Tonya, you knew I was married when we reconnected on Facebook. You could see my whole profile and you could even see Kim's profile. None of that stopped you from getting into this relationship with me. Your morals were not there then. I mean, I'm not trying to be funny, but you are already pregnant. There is no sense in trying to be righteous about it now. We just have to play this out and make it better from this point on."

"Carl, you are right. I did know that you were married. I loved and missed you so much that I only saw an opportunity to have what I wanted. I didn't consider your wife when I was in the throes of passion and God knows the last thing I wanted to do was get pregnant by you a second time. But I thank God for this pregnancy because it has opened my eyes to life and it's teaching me how to be a woman of morals. Based on that, there is no way that I can have this baby. We can't have a life together because you already have a family. When you leave your wife, you leave your children too. One thing you don't do is leave a child to go take care of another. Those children will need you just as much as this baby will. It's the right thing to do, Carl. Stay there with your wife and kids. I will get rid of this baby to help take some of the pressure off of you. It's one of the hardest decisions that I've ever had to make, which is why you need to leave me alone about it. Just let me do what I intend to do and please don't make me feel guilty about it."

"You don't want to have my baby?" he asked.

"Carl don't ask me that. It's not fair," Tonya said.

"Tell me you don't want my baby. If this is true, I will call of this whole thing off and go home. I'll never bother you again."

"I love you so much. It's true and it would be a dream come true to be the mother of your child, but this is bigger than us. We need to consider how all parties will be affected if we go through with this. I can't be a part of hurting innocent people. None of them deserves this. It's just not fair to them."

"So, if it's a dream come true, then why can't you just let this happen. I promise you I will work this out. We will be together. Me, you and the baby."

"Carl, that can never be. I mean, even if you were divorced, you still have two other children."

"I just want to be with you. We can include my other two. Do you love me enough to be a mother to all of my children."

"I love you enough to do way more than just be a mother to your children, but that's not what's right and it's not about love here."

"Love is all that it's about. Tonya, please don't kill my baby."

"That's a little melodramatic, Carl, don't you think?"

"Yes, but that's what you are going to do?"

"It's not a baby yet. I can get it before it starts developing."

"No, it is a baby. And it's a baby that we created together. Just give me some time to work this out and I promise that we will be together."

"Carl, I can't. My conscience is already messed up just knowing what we've already done. I can't make this any worse. I won't make this any worse."

"It won't be worse. I'm going to make it, so she leaves me."

"What?"

"I promise you that I won't walk out on her. When this is all said and done, Kim will be the person walking away from the marriage. She won't even want to look at me again."

"No, I can't let you do that. I can't be a part of it."

"You won't be. All you have to do is make sure we have a healthy baby. That means all you have to do is continue doing what you've been doing and just give me some time."

"When you say sometimes? What do you mean? How much time?"

"Two weeks. That's all that I need."

"I don't know about this, Carl. What are you going to do? Don't do something stupid to hurt that girl."

"I'm not and I won't, I promise. I'm going to make this as painless as possible. I mean our relationship has been on the rocks for years. I think she just needs a good reason to walk away from it all. She will be totally happy walking away with her children. I mean, she might fight for a few material things, but she will be the one leaving the marriage. I promise that I will not make this any worse than it needs to be."

"Carl?"

"Tonya, Baby. I'm asking you to trust me. I know you really don't have reason to and that I'm asking for a lot, but please give me an opportunity. I want nothing more than to wake up to you on a daily basis. Give me a chance. Please don't get rid of the baby, and in two weeks, I will be here with you. We will go through this pregnancy together. It's our baby so, it's we who are pregnant."

"Carl, I don't know if I can."

"You can and you will," he said, as he watched tears well up in her eyes. He saw her trying to fight as they welled up on the ends of her lower eyelids. He knew that if she blinked, they would flood down her face. He could see her doing everything in her power to stop them from falling.

"I love you, probably more than I should, especially with our given history. I always get so weak around you. I don't know how to say no to you. Please don't put me in this position," Tonya cried as tears began falling down her face.

Carl also had tears in his eyes, and they welled up as he realized that she was going to wait for him.

"I'm here baby. I'm not going anywhere. I promise. Please don't do it," he said, taking her into his arms.

"Okay, I'll wait for you. I won't get rid of it." Tonya placed her head on his chest as she wrapped her arms around him. "I have waited so long for this day. You have no idea how much I have dreamed of the day when you would say all of those words to me."

"Thank you so much. You are so beautiful. I thought so the moment that I met you and I believe it even more strongly now. You are just as beautiful inside, as you are outside. I am going to make sure that the light inside of you never goes out. I'm going to shower you with so much love. You watch and see."

"I hear you."

"I know you hear me, but do you believe me?"

"I do. I believe you and I will be right here whenever you get back. Me and the baby."

Carl picked his phone up from the couch and sent a text machine to Tonya.

Where are you? I've been looking for you for the past hour," he texted. He waited. When he got no response, he texted again.

Please answer me. I'm worried about you. He waited again.

Please don't do anything crazy. I just need you to give me a few more hours and I promise you that I will be there, he wrote.

He placed the phone back on the couch and as he noticed that it was six o'clock and that it was time for Cindy to arrive. He took a deep breath and walked to the stairs. He paused and looked up the stairwell.

"It's time," he said. "Let's get it." He climbed the stairs slowly. As he neared the top, he heard the doorbell ring.

"Showtime," he said.

TARA MONTGOMERY

PART FOUR

TARA MONTGOMERY

12 GAME TIME

The doorbell rang and Kimberly opened her eyes. She knew that it was Cindy arriving. She received a text from her a few minutes earlier notifying her that kids were back at her mother's house and were playing Xbox. Cindy also told Kim that she was on her way. After she received the text message, she waited patiently in her bedroom. She tried to meditate for the twenty minutes that it took Cindy to arrive at their front door. She wanted to be totally relaxed, so she can focus and play her role to the best of her ability. Carl had to believe that she was really upset about what was about to go down. He had to know that she was totally fed up, so he would agree to whatever she wanted, right away.

Kimberly stood up from the bed and walked toward the bedroom door. She looked around the room one last time. She knew that things were about to change. Life as they knew it would be no more from this day forward. She was going to be a single woman; free to do whatever she wanted. She would no longer have to wonder when she was going to be hurt or betrayed again. She wouldn't have to worry about trying to hide her tears from her children. No longer would she have to deal with puffy eyes in the morning after having cried all night. She would miss no more days from work because of those puffy eyes. Kim looked in the mirror that was on the dresser near the door. She noticed that her hair had held up well today. Her twist out had made it through all the twists and turns of this day. She walked out of the bedroom and down the stairs.

When she reached the bottom of the landing, she saw Carl walk past her and toward the front door. She stood where she was and watched him answer the door. He looked through the window to the side of the door and then unlocked it. He opened the door and ushered Cindy into the house.

Kim looked at Cindy and smiled. Carl could not see her because he still faced the door, and his back was to Kimberly. Kim nodded at Cindy and Cindy nodded back.

"Cindy, what are you doing here?" Kim asked.

Carl turned to face the two women as he closed the door. Cindy looked at Carl.

"Do you want to tell her, Carl?" Cindy

asked.

"Tell me what, Carl?" Kim asked.

"Cindy's here to see me."

"To see you for what? And where are my kids?"

"The kids are fine," Cindy said.

"What the hell do you mean the kids are fine?" Where are they and who are they with?"

"The kids are at the hotel like we said earlier," Cindy responded.

"At the hotel. What hotel and with who? You can't just drop my kids off at a random hotel with God knows who. And did I hear him say that you are here to see him. See him to do what?"

"She's who I picked for the grand opening," Carl said.

"Carl, you dirty son of a bitch. I should have known that you would do something dirty like this. But I'm going to have to get back to you later. Cindy, I asked you who you left my kids with?"

"They are with a reliable person. They are with my niece."

"Didn't you say earlier that your mother wasn't going to allow your niece to sit with the kids? I see why now. If I knew that you were trying to leave them so you could come over here, I would have told you to forget it. You should be happy that I'm not whipping your ass right now. This is not going down because you are about to go to that hotel to get my kids and bring them home."

"No, she is not. She's going to stay here and visit with me. Kim, what's wrong with you. We been planning this all day and we already said that you couldn't trip over who I bring here."

"That's before I knew that it was this bitch. Not only is she ratchet for being here, but she left my kids, who she is supposed to be babysitting, to come here so she could have sex with a married man."

"I know you didn't just call me a bitch."

"Yes bitch, I did. Are you crazy? Did you really think that I was just going to let you come in here and have sex with my man and not say anything?"

"Kim, we already said that we could pick whoever we wanted," Carl said.

"Carl, we said no friends."

"Cindy is not your friend. I've never seen you hang out with her. You don't even mention her until you need her to watch the kids. What you have is a business relationship."

"You call it what you want, but this is someone that we know. We said it can't be anyone that we share mutual friends with."

"No, that is not what we said. We said we don't want mutual friends to know. I know Cindy can keep a secret. Plus, I been wanting to get at her for years."

Kimberly looked at Cindy.

"If you don't get the hell out of my house, I promise you that you are not going to be happy in the next few minutes."

Kimberly watched as Cindy looked at her phone and read a text.

"Whoever you're talking to, you need to tell them to get over here because I'm already tired of this scene. They need to come and save you," Kim said, giving Cindy the okay to tell Tonya that it was safe to come on over.

"Kim, you need to calm down. Nobody is going anywhere. Cindy and I are going downstairs and there's nothing that you can do about it. We are going to wait here for your friend to arrive and then we will all be going our separate ways."

"First of Carl, you don't get to tell me what I can or cannot do. You are going to get this bitch out of my house, or you are going to get some of what she's about to get. I've had enough of your bull. I should have known that you had some dirty mess up your sleeve. There's no way you can do something like this with integrity. I should have known not to trust you. You have disappointed me at every opportunity, and I knew that this wasn't going to be any different. I don't know why I let you talk me into this."

"Talk you into this; you came up with this all by yourself. All I did was help you go through with it. If you hadn't mentioned it, I would have never thought of it. So, live with the bed that you made for yourself. Pull the covers back and take a nap. It won't be long."

"Pull the covers back and take a nap. I got your nap," she said as she lunged like she was going to hit him.

Cindy jumped in front of her and stopped her.

"Get your damn hands off of me," she snapped at Cindy.

"Look, this does not have to get out of hand." Cindy said. We are all consenting adults here."

"Consenting? Did you use that word to let me know that you have consented to have sex with my husband, with me in the house?"

"It's not like you didn't know what was going down before I got here and last I checked, you were okay with the whole thing before you knew that it was with me."

"You're right I was, but that was before I knew that you were a trifling whore."

"Okay, I'm not going to just stand here and let you call me all kinds of names."

"That's fine, then leave and bring my kids while you're at it. This is not going down today and definitely not in my house."

"This is going down. Stop it, Kim. You need to take it like a woman. It shouldn't make a difference who it is. We all agreed to this. Why can't you just put your big girl panties on and get over this."

"You know what, Carl? You're right," she said. "I did agree to this. But I didn't know that my kids would be involved and used as pawns."

"How am I using your kids as pawns?" Cindy asked. "I love your children."

"No, you don't. You just used them so you could get next to my husband. Well, you know what? You can have him. I'm done. I don't want his ass anymore."

"Wait a minute, slow down, Kim. You are taking this way too far," Carl said.

"Am I, Carl? You were right. We should have broken up a long time ago. You can get with her anywhere you want. I don't care. Just know that this marriage is finished. I'm not doing it anymore. I've had enough. No more."

"Kim, wait. This is not what we said. We said we were going to stick it out together."

"Together, you call this together. This is not together. Of all the women on the planet, you couldn't find anyone else. You had to find someone I would have to continue to see whenever I needed a babysitter. You didn't think that that would be awkward for her or for me?"

"No, I didn't. But I still don't see why it has to be awkward. She won't tell anyone and it's not like we are going to be in a relationship or anything like that."

"As usual, you are unbelievable. Like I said, do whatever you want. I'm not dealing with your mess anymore."

"Kim, I don't want to lose you. Not like this."

Kim felt her phone vibrate and she noticed that Cindy was looking at her phone as well. She looked at the phone and read the text.

I'm outside, Tonya wrote. Kim saw that the text went to her and Cindy. Cindy responded.

Wait two minutes and then come in.

"It's too late for that now, Carl. You do whatever you want. Cindy, you're fired once you get my kids back here. I never want to see you again."

"Kim, I can't believe that you're making such a big deal about this. It doesn't have to be this serious. Why can't we just go on with things as planned? "

"Because you broke the rules. That means all bets are off."

"Look, Carl. Kim might be right. This is too much now. I didn't expect her to react like this. I was only trying to help you guys out. I didn't intend to hurt anyone. You said that she was okay with this."

"What? You said what? You told her that I knew."

"Yes, I told her that you were okay with the grand opening," Carl said.

"But you didn't tell me that it was her. I knew I should have asked you who you chose but I figured it was going to be some skank that I didn't know. I'll tell you that Cindy was the last person that I expected," Kim lied. She knew that if this was going to really happen, that Cindy would be the first that he chose. Kim knew that he had been watching her for years and they had even had numerous arguments about her.

"Come on, Kim, let's be real. You knew I liked her."

"Yes, Carl I did, but I thought she was included in the no-friends rule. She was part of the reason why I suggested it."

"Well, then you know me, and this shouldn't be surprising to you. And once again, she is not a friend. She's the babysitter."

"Same difference. She's someone we know and deal with on a daily basis."

Kimberly stood with her hands on her hips and looked at the two of them; she knew that Carl was in panic mode and was curious how he was going to handle part two of this situation. She knew that she had him right where she wanted him.

The doorbell rang and all three turned to the door.

"So, what are you going to do now? You going to turn your friend away too?" Carl asked.

"Yep, because this is over. It's not going to happen," Kim said as she walked to the door.

13 STRANGE ENDINGS

Kimberly was very upset and this is exactly the way Carl wanted to see her. He knew that when she saw Cindy come through the door, that she would lose her mind. He had not planned for his children to be with Cindy while all of this was going on, but it had worked out in his favor. The idea that Cindy had left the children with someone else so she could come to their house for sex was priceless. Carl could not have planned it better himself. He wanted Kim to be upset, so one of two things could happen. She would either leave him or he would turn the tables on her and leave her after she finished the actual grand opening. He would use it against her, stating that this was one more thing that he could not get pass. Ultimately, it was his plan to be with Tonya before the night was over.

Carl could not see the person that stood outside as Kimberly opened the door. He had to admit that he was curious as to whom she could have chosen. He thought of asking her earlier but realized that he really didn't care to know. It did not make a difference which man was coming to his home because he knew that Kim would be so frustrated when she saw Cindy that she would lose her mind and not want to go through with the grand opening anyway. He knew that she would overreact, and he was even counting on it.

"Hey, so glad you're finally here," Kim said to the person outside the door.

Carl looked over at Cindy, who was trying to see who was standing on the other side of the door. He waited to hear the response of the person outside, but the person said nothing. He continued to listen as he also waited for Kimberly to tell the man that they had called off the grand opening and that he should leave, but the conversation never happened.

"Would you like to come in?" Kimberly asked.

She stepped aside to let the person into the door.

Surprised that Kimberly was inviting the man in, Carl put his head down and stared at his feet. He didn't want it to show on his face that he was confused by her behavior. After the person stepped inside, Kimberly closed the door. From his peripheral vision Carl noticed something familiar, yet strange. He noticed a pair of shoes that looked familiar to him. He had recognized the shoes, but he was not sure as to why they made him feel uncomfortable. After a moment, it dawned on him that not only were the shoes familiar, but they were women's shoes. Afraid to look up, he continued to stare down at his own feet. He realized that he knew who the shoes belonged to and hoped that the person standing in his home was not who he thought it was.

"Looks like we are all here," Kimberly said.

Carl let his eyes trail up the body of the woman standing in front of him. When his eyes arrived on her face, he became confused. He was at a loss for words. He stared into Tonya's face, asking questions without saying a word. He wanted to ask her what she was doing there and how she knew his wife? Was she there to participate in the grand opening or was this some kind of set up to get him? Carl stood staring at Tonya with his mouth open.

"What's going on, Kim?" He finally asked.

"What do you mean, Carl? We are having the grand opening. You already know what's going on?"

"How can we be having a grand opening? You don't have anyone here."

"Yes, I do. Tonya's here for me," Kim smiled. "Ain't that right, Sweetie?"

"Yes, that's correct," Tonya smiled back at

her.

Carl looked at Tonya again with a pleading, yet confused look.

"What's the matter, Carl? You don't want me to get with a woman. I figured this would be a lot easier for you to handle. I mean, you said you were having a hard time dealing with the idea of another man having being inside me. So, this is a less a bitter pill for you to swallow."

"This is not funny, Kim. Quit playing with me."

"No one's playing with you, Carl. This is how it's going down. Do you have a problem with it? I mean, you did just say that we could pick who we wanted right."

"This is not right; Kim and you know it. She's not even a man."

"When did we establish that the person had to be from the opposite sex?"

"I didn't think that we needed to, some things are just a given."

"Oh, I'm sorry, baby. I don't think I got that memo."

"This is not happening," Carl said.

"Why not, Carl? You were okay with Cindy, so it should be fine with Tonya, right? Plus, we don't have to worry about her falling in love with me because she's not gay; she's just curious like I am."

"Kim, stop it. This is not funny. I need you

to go get your real choice."

"Carl, this is my real choice. I'm not joking. This is not a game. Tonya is here as my grand opening date."

Carl could not bring himself to look at Tonya, whom he could feel was staring directly into his face. He hoped that this was just a joke and that they would all bust out laughing at any minute. He wanted to ask Tonya to explain this whole situation, but he didn't know if it was wise for him to let Kim know that he knew Tonya.

"Look, just a minute ago, you wanted to call the whole thing off. Now she shows up at the door and it's back on. It's apparent that we need to rethink this whole thing."

"You know, Carl. I could say the same for you. A minute ago, you were adamant about going through with this thing and now you see that it's a woman and you want to call it off."

"It's because I know that you're not gay and that you are making a farce of this whole thing."

"I'm not making a farce. I'm just as serious about this as you are."

"Carl let's just go downstairs like we planned, and they can stay up here and work this out between them. Who Kim decides to sleep with is her own business," Cindy said.

"Oh, no, the hell you didn't," Kim said. "You need to just shut up and mind your own business. You better be happy that I'm still considering this, knowing what you're trifling ass is up to."

"I'm not up to anything. Carl told me about your little grand opening, and I thought it was a good opportunity, so I took it, to be truthful."

"To be truthful. What the hell are you talking about? What good opportunity?"

"I know that he's been watching me for as long as I've worked for you guys. I knew it was only a matter of time before he would make his move."

"Carl, you better get this bitch before I reach over and snatch her damn eyes out of her head."

Carl continued to stare into Tonya's face. He did not interfere in the argument between the other two women. He could not get over the fact that she was there, in his home. If he were going to take anyone anywhere, it wouldn't be Cindy. It would be Tonya. He wanted to grab her hand and drag her downstairs so he could get to the bottom of the whole mess. Carl realized at this point that he would have to get Tonya away from Kim, so he could ask her a few questions.

"There is too much going on here," Carl said with his eyes still trained on Tonya. "What do you have to say about all of this?"

"Who me?" Tonya asked, speaking for the

first time since she entered the house.

"Yes, doesn't any of this bother you? He asked.

"I'm not sure what's going on," she said.

"What don't you know?" Kim asked. "There's nothing more to know other than what you came here for."

"I guess," Tonya said, looking at Carl.

"I know this all has to be uncomfortable to you. You don't have to stand around and listen. You could just say forget the whole thing and we would all understand," Carl said.

"No, we won't understand. She's not leaving. She's going to do what she came here to do. So go ahead, Tonya."

"What do you mean, go ahead, Tonya?"

"She's right," Tonya said. "I should just do what I came here for. It's the only thing to do."

"Thank you," Cindy said. "It's about time somebody said something with some since, but I don't know how she became the deciding factor."

"Oh, I've been the deciding factor. Ain't that right, Carl? This whole thing has been centered around me from the very beginning, right Carl?" Tonya asked.

"What?" Carl responded.

"We are all here for you actually, right?"

"I don't know what you're talking about. I didn't even know that you were coming here," he said.

"What do you mean you didn't know she was coming here? Do you know her, Carl?" Kim asked.

"No, I don't," he lied. He was confused and still unsure of how he should answer the question.

"Of course, you know me, Carl. We go way back, don't we," Tonya said.

"Oh shoot," Cindy said. "This is about to get good."

"Shut the hell up, Cindy," Carl snapped.

"Why does she have to shut up, Carl?" Kimberly asked. "She's right; this is about to get good."

"No, it's not. Tonya, let me talk to you in private," he said.

"So, you do know her?" Kimberly asked.

"Of course, he knows me. Go ahead, Carl. Tell them. Tell the truth."

Carl looked at all three women as they waited for him to speak. He did not know what to say. He realized that he was in a tight situation, and he understood that he had been set up.

"You know what? I'm not about to do this with any of you," he said, walking away from the front door and into the house.

"Oh, you are going to do this. Right here and right now," Tonya said. "You are going to tell them about us. Tell them about our history and how it's repeated itself in our present."

"Our? Carl why does she keep referring to the two of you as our?"

"Because we have a shared life. Our paths keep seeming to cross every few years or so and this time; they are a bit more intertwined."

"What is she talking about?" Kim asked.

"Tonya, please don't do this here, baby," he said.

"Baby, did you just call her baby?"

"That's what you call the woman that's pregnant with your child right, Carl?" Tonya asked.

"Pregnant?" Kim and Cindy said at the same time.

"Okay, this isn't my scene. I'm not trying to be involved in no family drama. This is not what I signed up for. I'm out of here."

Carl looked over a Cindy. He did not care that she was leaving. She was the least of his worries. He was only using her as a ploy to make Kim angry. She could and should leave so he could deal with this Tonya situation.

"That's fine, Cindy girl and thank you for your help," Kim said.

"Help? You knew about this. You set me up?" Carl asked Cindy.

"Of course I did. I think it's real messed up that you would try to get with me knowing that

Kim and I were cool. I mean, I spend the night in your home, and she trusts me with her children. That would be low of me as a woman to betray her and sleep with her man. She knew about your shenanigans from the very beginning. We just had to find a way to call you on it all."

Carl looked back at Kim who crossed her arms and looked at him with a smug look on her face.

"This is not about, Cindy. This is about you and me," Tonya said.

"Wait, you know Cindy too?"

"I didn't initially but we met recently in the planning of this. So, let's just get this all out in the open. Seems like there's been a whole lot of lying going on around here."

"Tonya don't do this. We had a plan. This could all be over right here and right now. We don't need to ruin it. We can have everything we've ever wanted. We can be together now, and you don't have to worry about me being with anyone else."

"Oh really," Kim said. "So, you really think that it's going to be that easy. I am not letting you off the hook that fast."

"Me either. At least not until you tell Kim the whole truth," Tonya said.

"Is that what it's going to take?" He asked Tonya.

"Yep," she said.

"Okay, if that's the way it's got to be," Carl said. He knew that it was time for him to man up and tell his wife the truth. He could no longer live with the guilt of what he had done to Tonya so many years ago. This was his chance to clear the air, get a clean slate, and have a chance at real happiness.

"I met Tonya many years ago. We used to kick it and she got pregnant. The problem was at that time; I wasn't ready to be a father so, I talked her into having an abortion. She didn't want to do it, but I told her that we would try again in a few years and that we would get married. Of course, she believed me and agreed to the abortion. On the day that she was scheduled to have the procedure, I told her that I would be there with her when she went through it. We went down to the clinic and when they took her back to the room, I couldn't take it and I left. I never saw her again, until years later."

"You sorry excuse for a man," Kim said as she watched the tears run down Tonya's face. "You just left her there to go through that alone?"

"I couldn't do it. It was too much to handle."

"Too much to handle? Are you kidding me? You thought it was too much to handle, so you left me there to handle it by myself?"

"Tonya, I told you that I am sorry for that. I was young—a kid. I didn't know what to do. I haven't been able to live with myself ever since. I've lived with it for the past ten years. That's why I've been trying to make it up to you all these months."

"All these months?" Kim said. "How long has she been back in your life?"

"For the past eleven months," Tonya responded.

"Yes, and now she's pregnant again," Carl said. "And I am not going to let her go through any of it alone. She's going to have my baby and I am going to be right by her side when she does."

"Unbelievable, you're joking right?" Kim asked.

Carl was beginning to feel better since he was finally able to tell Kim the truth. She deserved to know what was going on and he was getting tired of keeping the secret.

"I love Tonya and I always have. I knew that even back then, but I was too young to deal with those feelings. Guys didn't fall head over hills for the first girl that they ever had sex with. I was supposed to be a player like the rest of my friends. I couldn't let my friends know that I had slipped up. It was just an adolescent mistake that I've spent most of my adult life trying to fix."

"Well, for me, it was the most heartbreaking thing that I've ever experienced. I haven't been able to trust anyone since. Initially, I just wanted you to come back and make it all better. I thought about coming to find you, but I didn't think that I could ever look you in the face. Plus, I had a hard time trying to forgive myself for letting you trick me into giving you my heart and body. I felt so stupid. After the years past, I went from sadness to total anger. You needed to pay for what you've done to me, and I was not going to stop until I figured out a way to get you back."

"Well, it's good that you got past that. Now we can be together and raise our child."

"Not exactly," Kimberly said, interrupting his private moment with Tonya. "Don't you remember, Tonya came here to see me."

"What are you talking about, Kim? You can't let the act go. It's all out in the open now," Carl said.

"Not exactly," Tonya said. "I did come here to see, Kim.

"What does that mean?" He asked.

"It means that you've been played and she's not pregnant."

"What?" Carl asked, looking at Tonya.

"Nope, not at all. There's no baby. I just wanted you to suffer like I did. I told you it became my life's mission to make you pay for what you did to me. So not only did I take away your baby, like you took away mine, but I am also taking away your marriage."

"What are you saying? You and Kim are a couple?"

"Hell no," Kimberly said. "I don't like women."

"Then what are you talking about?"

"Well, based on all of this, I've decided that I'm leaving you and I'm taking my children. You will no longer hurt me and make me feel guilty about what you're doing."

"So, what does this have to do with Tonya?" He asked.

"As far as you and I are concerned, nothing, but she's my cousin who I haven't seen in twenty years. My mother put us back in touch and when she found out that you were my husband and what you had been putting me through for the past ten years, we decided that it was time to make you pay."

"Kim, you know our marriage was finished years ago. So, this does not hurt me at all."

"Yes, but I know that you are destroyed that you can't have your precious Tonya."

"Man, I don't care about either one of you bitches," he lied. He was destroyed that Tonya could do something like this to him. He wanted to fall on his knees and plead for her forgiveness, but he knew that it wouldn't work. He knew that karma would come back around and visit him one day, but he had no idea that it would be like this. He was not only losing Tonya, but he also lost her baby, and he would now lose his home and children. "This is over. I hope you both had fun."

"Oh, we did," Tonya said. Carl could see that there was still hurt in her eyes. He knew that if Kim was not in the room, that he would be able to convince her to take him back. He wanted nothing in the world but to be with Tonya.

"Sure did," Kim responded.

Carl looked back and forth between the two women. He knew that there was nothing he could do in this present situation to change either of their minds. He had to just accept his fate for the time being and try to regroup later. As much as he wanted to explain his situation to both women, he knew that he would never be able to get them to understand that he just didn't know how to express himself. He didn't mean to hurt people; he just didn't know how to handle it when the feelings got all mixed and bottled up. He walked to the small closet near the front door, grabbed his jacket and walked out the front door. He needed to go somewhere with less estrogen, so he could get his head right. He jumped into his car and drove away.

TARA MONTGOMERY

14 RUDE AWAKENINGS

The ringing of her cell phone caused Kimberly to wake from her sleep. She did not realize that she had fallen asleep. She was waiting the last few minutes until the participants of the grand opening arrived. She had just laid back on the bed and closed her eyes to calm her nerves. She wanted to be in the best mind space when it was time to put her plan into action. Now she was being awakened by what she thought was real life. She had just dreamed that both ladies had arrived and the three of them together, had ganged up on Carl. The plan had gone so well that not only did she tell him that she was leaving him, but he even lost his side chick. Kimberly had felt so vindicated and was now beginning to feel disappointed that it was all just a dream. She realized that her dream was a visual representation of what she had hoped would happen.

She picked her phone up off the bed with one hand and rubbed her eyes with the other.

"Hello," she said after sliding the bar over to answer the phone.

"Kim, I can't do it."

"What? Wait, who is this?"

"It's Cindy. You don't know my voice?"

"Oh, yes. I know your voice. I was just sleeping. I'm sorry," Kim said.

"Okay. Well, anyway, did you hear what I said? I said I cannot do it."

"You can't do what, Cindy?"

"I can't go through with it. I can't have sex with your husband. That would be disloyal to my boyfriend."

"Cindy, you don't have a boyfriend," Kimberly responded.

"No, not exactly, but my ex and I have been talking about getting back together. I don't want to do anything to jeopardize that."

"Cindy let's be serious. What's really going on?"

"I just told you. I can't do it. I don't want to hurt anyone."

"Hurt who? Who are you worried about hurting?"

"I don't know, Kim. You and Carl. Hell, maybe even myself. I'm the only person that has to live with me, when this all said and done."

"Look Cindy, I'm not asking you to fall in love with guy. I just want you to sleep with him so I can have grounds to walk away when it is all said and done."

"And what happens to me, Kim? Have you considered how your little rendezvous would affect the people that you intertwine?" Cindy asked.

"Yes, I have considered it. You would be having consensual sex that would just be a one-night stand. I didn't ask you to marry anyone. Not to mention that you aren't in a relationship at the moment, which is part of the reason why I was happy that he chose you."

"And Carl?"

"What about Carl?" Kimberly asked.

"You are so hell bent on getting back at him. Did you consider what this might do to him?"

"What, what might do to him?"

"He's about to lose his entire family. Don't you think that's going to be devastating?"

"It could be, but I don't care. My intention is to hurt him as much as he's been hurting me."

"Well, that's just vindictive and childish and I decided that I don't want to be a part of any of it. I can't live with knowing that I was the cause of the breakup of a family."

"No one will be the cause of Carl losing his family. The only one that will be blamed for it is

Carl. He brought all of this on himself. He should have thought about the possibility of losing his family when he was out there doing all those things to hurt me and to break my heart."

"Well, regardless. Like I said earlier, I can't do it and I will not do it. I will not drop my integrity for you or anyone else."

"Wow, this is unbelievable."

"I'm sorry. Oh, and there's one more thing. I called Tonya and told her that I wasn't going to do it, so I don't think she's going to do it either."

"So, you convinced my cousin not to help me."

"No, she's a grown woman and she needs to make up her own mind. I just told her about my views on it and she agreed. She should be calling you here shortly, too."

"So, does Carl know that you're not coming?"

"I sent him a text."

"Did he respond?" Kimberly asked.

"Not yet, but I've also been on the phone with you since I texted him."

"So, what are we supposed to do if you two aren't going to show up?"

"I don't know, do like most people and work out your differences or break up. But either way, handle it like adults and don't involve others in your mess."

As much as Kimberly wanted to be angry with Cindy and Tonya, she knew that Cindy was right. She should have been a better person in the way she chose to handle this situation. Her heart had just gotten the best of her, and she just wanted to see Carl suffer, even if it was only for just a short while.

"So, you can go ahead and bring my children home since you are not coming," Kimberly said.

"I'll bring them home tomorrow like we planned. Plus, that would require me to show up there tonight and I don't intend to show my face there until tomorrow. I'm quite sure you can come up with a reason for why I didn't take them to the hotel as planned, incase Carl asked. I can also bring the money that he gave me tomorrow," Cindy said.

"Look, don't worry about the money. You are right. I should have a better way of handling things. And if I was going to try to use having an opening relationship, then maybe I should have done just that. I should have invited a man to come over here and to have sex with me."

"Or you could just tell your husband how you really feel. Kim, you have something that many other women are trying to get. I realize that you might not have the best husband but at least you have one. He's there for your children and that's the most important part of it all, isn't it? I'm not trying to tell you how to handle your marriage and I am definitely not trying to interfere with the decisions that you make concerning your marriage, but I just don't feel like involving others into your mischief is the answer. I truly am sorry, Kim."

"It's all good, Cindy and thank you for calling. You didn't have to."

"No, I did have to. I owed you that. I've been feeling like this ever since you asked me to do this. I should have spoken up then."

"Well, I got it. I need to get downstairs to see how he's going to handle this. I'm quite sure he's not going to be happy."

"Okay, well, I'll see you tomorrow when I bring the kids back."

"Okay, I'll talk to you later."

Kimberly ended the call and stared into the emptiness of the room. She felt like all that she had worked for to make sure Carl got what he deserved had come crashing down on her at the last minute. There was no way she could call anyone else.

She took a deep breath and walked toward the bedroom door. She slowly walked toward the stairs and reluctantly walked down. As she was going, her phone rang again. She looked at the screen and realized that it was Tonya calling now. She turned and headed back up the stairs.

"Hello," Kimberly said as she returned to

the bedroom.

"Kim, hey girl."

"What's up, Cuz? How are you?"

"I'm good. I'm just having second thoughts."

"I know. I just got off the phone with Cindy. She told me that she talked to you."

"Yeah, she called and told me that she wasn't going to do it and she thought that I shouldn't do it either."

"I mean, some of the stuff she said, I agree with. She had a few valid points, but we went through a lot to plan this thing and it's just jacked up that it's not going to happen."

"Well, I never said that I wasn't coming. I just said that I'm having second thoughts."

"Did you call Carl yet?"

"No, and I don't plan on it. He needs to be in panic mode for all that he's done to me."

"You know he probably thinks that you're down at the abortion clinic."

"I know. He's still blowing up my phone. Sending text messages telling me to hold on for a few more hours," Tonya laughed. "It's so pathetic."

"It sure is, but he is doing this to himself, which is why this has to happen."

"I hear you. I can still come but it won't be the same without Cindy."

"That's fine. He wanted to get screwed, so

we are still going to make sure that it happens. In our own way of course," Kimberly laughed as well. "But I don't want you to come at the planned time. Give me thirty extra minutes. I want to give him an opportunity to come clean and tell me the truth. Which I know he won't do."

"Of course, he won't, girl. He's had plenty of opportunities and many years to tell you about me and our relationship."

"It's so sad."

"Okay, so I'll see you in a little while. I'll let you know when I'm on my way."

"All right, bye."

Kimberly felt a sense of relief come over here. She was happy that Tonya was still going to come and help her achieve at least part of her plan. When Cindy changed her mind, Kim was confused as to what she was going to do. She thought that she might have had to call one of her male friends to actually come over and have sex. She knew a few men who would jump at the opportunity and had in fact put two of them on standby in case she changed her mind. She did not think that she would have to use them for an emergency change of plan.

She walked back out of the bedroom and down the two flights of stairs to the basement. Carl was sitting on the couch with his head in his hands. He did not seem to hear her enter the room, or he did not care that she was there?

"What's the matter?" Kimberly asked. "Is everything okay?"

Carl said nothing. He just kept his head in his hands.

"Carl, do you hear me? Are you all right?"

"Not right now, Kim," he said through his hands.

"What? What do you mean not right now? It's almost time. The people should be here in the next few minutes. You need to get yourself together."

Carl ignored her again. She knew that he was worried because Cindy wasn't coming. Kimberly continued to press him.

"Well, you know, if you want to call this thing off like I said earlier, then I'm open to that. It's not that big of a deal. We can just do it another time."

"Kim, please just stop it. I need you to just go away for a minute."

"Go away? I'm not going anywhere. We are in this together, remember? Why don't you just tell me what's going on?"

"Nothing's going on, Kim. I just got some things on my mind."

"Well, maybe if you tell me about it, I can help you come up with a solution or something."

"I can handle this on my own," Carl said,

quickly rising from his seat and raising his voice at the same time.

"What the hell is wrong with you? What are you yelling at me for? I didn't do anything to you. I'm only trying to help," Kimberly yelled back.

"I just asked you to leave me alone for a few minutes. I mean, you can't even do that. That's why I don't want to be with you anymore. You never know when to back off," he said.

"Wait a minute," Kimberly said. "Did you just say that's why you don't want to be with anymore? Is that how you feel. You don't want to be with me, and you were about to let me do this open relationship thing with you, knowing that you had no intention of being with me."

"I never said that I wasn't going to be with you; I said I didn't want to be with you. Those are two different things."

"So, what are you saying? You were going to stay with me, even though you knew that this is not what you want."

"I made a promise, right?"

"Seriously? Is that you're logic?" Kim asked.

"Yes," he said.

"Unbelievable. You keep finding new ways to surprise me, which is odd because you do it all of the time. Which is why I don't know why some of the things that you say are so hard for me to believe."

"Whatever, Kim. I'm not in the mood to argue with you."

"That's fine because you don't have time. They are going to be here any minute now," Kim lied. She knew that Cindy was nowhere near where they lived, and that Tonya wasn't coming for at least another half hour.

"I have time. I just don't want to discuss this with you. My friend called and she's not coming. She is not going to be able to make it."

"What? So now what? Did you call someone else?"

"No, I didn't call anyone else. I just got the call, okay?"

"Is that why you were so upset when I came down here. You're in here stressing about some chick that won't come to give you some booty. I mean, really, is it the end of the world? I'm quite sure you know a whole lot of other whores that you can call."

"Kim, that's enough with all the whores."

"Why, Carl? That's all they can be if they are willing to come over here and have sex with a married man. I'm quite sure the person that was coming here knew you were married, but that didn't stop her or make her think twice."

Kimberly realized that she was happy that Cindy told her why she could not go through with the plan. She was able to use it in this argument with him to get the information that she needed.

"Look, she's not whore and you better stop calling her one."

"Whatever, Carl. Say what you want, and I will do the same."

"All right you want to play games, then let's do it. Let's get it started."

15 AND SURPRISE

"You want to play games, okay. Let's do it. The girl coming here wasn't a whore; she was."

"Who?" Kimberly said, cutting him off before he could finish his sentence. "Who is she?"

"If you be quiet long enough, I'll tell you. That's always been your problem; you talk too damn much and don't know how to listen. Sometimes, no most of the time, I just wish that you would just shut the hell up and let me hear myself think. You never know when to quit. I can't stand it anymore."

"Like I said, whatever," Kim said, blowing him off.

"Kim, the woman coming over here wasn't a whore," Carl said calmly. "It was Cindy."

"Cindy who?"

"The babysitter, Cindy."

"My Cindy," Kimberly asked.

"If that's how you want to refer to her, but yes, the Cindy that watches our children."

"And what was she coming over here to do?"

"What do you think she was coming over for? Stop asking stupid questions, Kim."

"So, she was coming over here to have sex with you?"

"Now you're getting it. It took you a little while but you're tracking now."

"And you think I was just going to stand here and let it happen."

"You could have tried to stop it but there wasn't anything that you could have done about it."

"Really?"

"Yes, really."

"I think not, Carl. And how was she going to come over here when she is supposed to be keeping my kids?"

"She had a plan."

"Oh, the hell no, she didn't. If she had shown up here without my kids, we would have had big problems. So, why did she change her mind? Why isn't she coming? Did she get scared?"

"You don't need to know why she's not coming. Just know that she won't be here."

"Aw, you sound so devastated," Kimberly laughed.

"Laugh all you want, but that is the least of your issues."

"What issues, Carl? I don't have any issues."
"Yes, you do."
"What issues do I have?"
"You are going to have to decide how you are going to live without me because I'm leaving you."
"And what does that mean?"
"It means exactly what I said. I'm leaving you and this marriage. I think I feel good that she didn't come because now I don't have to use it as a gimmick to leave you. I was only going through with this so I could use it against you afterwards. I was going to act like I was upset because you slept with another man again, so I could use it as grounds to walk away. But now I realize that I don't need a trick or a lie to get out of this. I just need to tell you the truth and the truth is, I don't want you anymore. I don't love you anymore and I can no longer live a lie. You will just have to figure out how to live your life without me. Just know that you brought this all on yourself. I realize that I was doing a lot of things that was breaking your heart, but then I realized that it was easy for me to do those things because I really wasn't concerned about your feelings. The problem is, I don't know when I started feeling like this. I do know that I have never loved you as much as I thought I did, and that realization hit me just recently. So, to some extent, I owe you an

apology because I have been living a lie for many years, but the upside is I've been displaying my true feelings for you through my behavior for a very long time. You were just so blinded by your dumb love for me that you could not see it or maybe you didn't want to see it. Either way, I'm letting you off the hook to find your way cause Lord knows I'm going to find mine. Don't worry, I'll be here for my kids, you can believe that. I'm leaving you but never my children, so don't try to use them against me like the rest of these crazy ass chicks out here. I will be involved in all aspects of their lives and if you don't like this or anything I'm saying I really don't care. Now, I'm done with this conversation, and you can say or do whatever you want. Now deal with it."

Carl turned and walked in the direction the bathroom. He could not believe he had said and done what he just did, and he needed to get away from her to regroup. As he took a few steps, he felt a sharp pain on the back of his head and fell to the floor. He grabbed his head and turned on to his back. He looked up and saw Kim standing over him.

"What the hell is wrong with you?" he asked. "Are you crazy?

"Hell no, I'm not crazy. Who the hell are you talking to? Don't you ever talk to me like that again. I am not a child, least of all not your child. I will truly kill you if you ever take to me like that again," Kimberly said, standing over him. "I have been letting you belittle me for far too long. I'm so over it. I might have to learn to live without you, but I promise you, I am so excited about it. I have been putting up with you all this time, just like you have put up with me. The difference is I thought that I was happy for some of it. I guess I know now that I wasn't. But you can believe that I am no longer brainwashed. You can leave me, and you can leave these kids, but while you're claiming them, please know that I am still their mother. I get the final say on all that goes on with them. You can see them, but all decisions are mine. There is one thing that I truly agree with you on, and it is dumb love. You are so right in your analysis of my dumb love for you. But I have learned, not only do I not love you, but there is nothing dumb about me when it comes to you anymore. So, please know that I am not scared of you on any level and if you ever disrespect me again, I'm going to go from dumb to crazy," Kimberly smiled down at him.

"I think you might already be there," Carl said, rubbing the spot where his head was hurting. "What did you hit me with?"

"My cell phone. It was the only thing that I could get my hand on at the moment and I had to get you before you made it to the bathroom.

I didn't think you would fall to the floor like a little girl."

"Don't ever hit me again. If you do, I'm going to forget that you are woman. That's all my saying.

"I don't have any more cell phones to throw," Kimberly said sarcastically.

Carl stood up while still rubbing his head.

"What the hell did you hit me with?" He asked again.

"I already told you, I hit you with my cell phone. It was what was in my hand during the heat of the moment."

"Doesn't make a difference what you do; this is still over," Carl said.

Just as he finished his statement, he heard the doorbell ring.

"I guess your friend is here," he said. "You might want to go and get that."

"I thought we were going to meet them together?" Kimberly asked.

"That was when we were both going to have someone here. Now, I don't care who's coming or what you are planning to do with him. It's not my concern anymore. You can go do anything that you want."

"Is that right?" Kimberly asked.

"Absolutely," Carl said, walking toward the bathroom.

"That's so childish, but of course, that's the

kind of person that you are. That's the kind of person that you've always been. I don't know why I ever expect anything different."

"Takes one to know one, woman. Also, you should remember that birds of the same feather flock together."

"Oh no, I don't think so, Carl. I'm nothing like you, thank God. I mean, if I was, I might have to kill myself," Kimberly retorted.

"Whatever Kim. Like I said, do whatever you want. I really don't care."

Carl walked into the bathroom and closed the door. He could hear Kimberly ascend the stairs. He heard the security alarm chime, indicating that she had opened one of the doors of the house. He sat on the edge of the tub as he heard two sets of footsteps coming back down the stairs. He had forgotten that Kimberly had decided to use the basement bedroom. He didn't want to come out of the bathroom, especially since he knew that he would have no one there to offset the situation. He was using Cindy to make Kimberly angry, but he had every intention of doing her just the same. That was going to be a freebee for him. He got to make Kimberly mad and get an orgasm all at the same time. This was supposed to be a win-win situation for him, but instead, here he was, hiding in the bathroom, wishing that this day would finally be over. He didn't want to go out and face whomever it was that Kimberly had invited over. He did not want to deal with Kimberly rubbing it in his face that she had someone there and he didn't. He knew that he had just told her that the relationship was over, but he had only done it at this moment, so she would not be able to get any gratification out of winning in the situation. He thought that if there was no relationship at all, the grand opening would be null and void. There can be no opening of the relationship if there was no relationship. It really was his intention to end the relationship, but he was desperate at the moment when Cindy told him that she wasn't coming. He had to do something to save face. He could not be made a fool of. That would give Kimberly something to talk about for years to come. Instead, the joke was on her. She lost her husband on the same night that was intended for her to save her marriage. It was such a cliché; he couldn't believe that he had thought of it so quickly and without any planning.

Carl smiled to himself at the thought of his own cleverness. He had to admit that there were times when he surprised and impressed himself. There were not many opportunities for him to accomplish such a feat but, this was one for the record books. He checked his hair and face in the mirror. It was time to meet this clown that she was bringing into his home. He would say his hellos and then he would leave to go and find Tonya. The thought of her brought a smile to his face. Carl had promised her that they would be together as of this very evening, and he was excited that he was going to be able to go to her and tell her that the mission had been accomplished. Overall, this was shaping up to be just as successful as he planned, and he didn't have to put any real effort into it. He would have to remember to thank Cindy in the morning when she brought the kids to him. Wait, he would not be there when she brought the kids. He grabbed the doorknob and walked out of the bathroom with his head held high.

"Here he comes now," he heard Kimberly say to her guest, whom he could not see because they were around the corner in the bar area. He did not know why his entrance had to be announced. Didn't Kimberly hear him say that he did not care whom she brought into the house anymore? Did she really think that he still wanted to meet the guy?

"Hey Carl," Kimberly said. "I want you to meet someone."

Carl stopped in his tracks and decided that he didn't want to see the man. He walked back to his pool table, reached down, picked up the triangle and started racking the ball into it.

"No thanks. It's none of my business," he

said.

"Yes, it is your business. We are still married. After the divorce, you can say that you don't care but right now you don't have a choice."

"Of course, I have a choice and I'm choosing not to come over there to meet your little friend."

"My little friend, huh?" Kimberly said. "Well, I guess we will just have to come over there to you.

Kimberly placed her hands on her hips and Carl turned his attention back to the pool table.

"So, you really don't want to meet my cousin?"

"What?" Carl asked.

"My cousin. She's here and she would really like to meet you," Kimberly said as Carl noticed a smug smile come across her face.

"What the hell are you talking about, Kim? I don't have time for your little kid games."

"Oh, this is not a game, Carl. I promise. You are really going to like meeting her."

Carl was about to reach for his pool stick but changed his mind and began to walk in the direction of where he knew the woman was standing.

"Why would I want to meet your cousin, especially a female cousin? She's here at the wrong time? You should have told her to come back," he said as he arrived near the couch where Kimberly was standing, his back still to the bar area.

"Don't worry about who's coming to see me; I got this. I just want to introduce you to her because this is your home too and it is common courtesy for all guests to speak to the owner when they arrive. Isn't that what we teach our children when they go visit their friends?"

"Whatever, Kimberly, save me the lecture."

"Kimberly, huh. That's nice. I believe that it's been years since you've called me by full name. It must mean that you are pretty upset. I think I like it though. It has a certain ring. I think I even detect a slice of envy."

"Envy, for what? You didn't do anything?"

"Envy for what is about to go down here."

"What's going down here? This is nothing outside of what was already planned. Do you think I'm envious because you get to go through with the plan, and I don't? You know I could get anyone that I want over here, but I'm just tired of playing this little cat and mouse game with you. I just don't have the patience for it anymore."

"That's fine, Carl. You don't need to have any more patience because I'm about to put an end to all of this once and for right here and right now. Are you ready?" Carl noticed a mischievous grin on her face.

"Am I ready for what? There's nothing to be ready for. Quit playing with me, Kim. I don't care who you got here or who your cousin is. Both of you can go away from here and just let me play my pool game in peace."

"You are going to have all the peace and quiet that you want in a little while, I promise, but let me just introduce you to my first cousin and then I'll leave you alone. Deal?"

"Not making and deals with you and I really don't care about you or your cousin."

"Well, I knew you would say something like that, so I'm just going to introduce you to her anyway. Carl, I want you to meet my cousin. Cousin, could you come over here and meet my husband."

The woman that stood in the bar area with her back to him turned and began walking toward him. Carl could not believe his eyes. He had to be in another dream. There is no way that he was seeing what he thought he was seeing. His eyes and mind had to be deceiving him. He had been thinking and worrying so much today that his mind had finally snapped. This had to be a hallucination.

"Carl, I would like for you to meet my cousin, Tonya Ellison. Tonya, meet my husband and your future baby daddy, Carl King."

Tonya walked over to him and placed her

hands on her hips.

"Hello Carl. How are you?"

Carl was at a loss for words. He could not believe that Tonya was not only in his home, but she was also here with his wife. Not only was she here with his wife, but also, she was being identified as his wife's cousin.

"Aren't you going to say hello, Carl?" Tonya said.

Carl let his body drop back on the couch as a look of surprise morphed on his face. He sat there staring at the two women.

"What's the matter, Carl?" Kimberly asked. "Cat got your tongue?"

Carl noticed that Kimberly had a little smug look on her face, but he did not stay focused on it very long. His eyes were fixated on Tonya, as he could not believe what was going on. He knew that these women were in cahoots to get him, and he knew that he needed to brace himself. He thought of getting up to leave and of ignoring this whole situation, but the fact that the women were there made him believe that that would be easier said than done. He would have to sit here and endure this situation. Take it like a man.

"Come on, Carl. Say something. I want you to. Hell, I need you because I know whatever is about to come out of your mouth is going to be priceless."

TARA MONTGOMERY

16 AND THE TRUTH SHALL SET YOU FREE

Kimberly reached up into the cabinet that was over the sink in the wet bar area. She pulled a glass down and filled it with water from the sink. She brought the glass to her lips and drank a few swallows of the water. She could feel the water go down her throat and penetrate her cells; she felt refreshed. She walked over to where Carl and Tonya stood.

"What's the matter, Carl? You look like you saw a ghost or something? Is something wrong?" Kimberly smiled.

"No, nothing is wrong. Why would something be wrong?" He answered.

"I don't know. You tell me. Is there something that you want to say?"

"Nope. Why would I?"

"You tell me. The way you're looking at my cousin here, it seems you have a lot to say."

"Are you sure you don't have anything to

say?" Tonya asked him.

"No, I don't. Apparently, the two of you think that I should have something profound to say, so why don't you tell me what you think I should be saying?" Carl said.

"Well, you can try hello. I said hello to you, and you said nothing. It's rude to let someone speak to you and you say nothing in return. I mean I am a guest in your home."

Kimberly watched as Carl stared into Tonya's face. She could tell that he knew exactly who she was by the look of recognition on his face.

"You might be a guest in my home but, you are not here to see me, so it doesn't make a difference if I speak to you or not. But since you're making such a big deal about it. Hello. How are you doing?"

"I'm doing fine. Thanks for asking."

"It's nice to meet you," Carl said seeming to be fishing for something from Tonya.

"Oh, come on, Carl. You know you don't mean that. Did you really just say it's nice to meet her?" Kimberly asked.

Carl did not respond to Kimberly's question and kept his eyes trained on Tonya. He seemed as if he was trying to say something to her without saying it to her.

"So, I hear that your friend is not going to make it today?"

"No, she can't make it," he said with a sense of relief.

"That's too bad. I was actually looking forward to meeting her?" Tonya said.

"Me too," Kimberly said.

"So, are you the person that was coming here for Kimberly for the grand opening?"

"Yes, does that surprise you?" Tonya said.

"Uh, yes," Carl said. "She did say that you were her cousin, right?"

"Yes, I am. Haven't you ever heard of kissing cousins?" Tonya asked. "I mean I really love my cousin."

"Wow, ok. I don't know what to say to that."

"You would be at a loss for words, wouldn't you Carl?" Kimberly laughed.

Carl turned his gaze to Kimberly for the first time since he noticed Tonya. His looked turned from confusion to anger. Kimberly could see that there were many thoughts that were running in his mind, but nothing came out of his mouth.

"You know Carl; I see you as my cousin too," Tonya said.

"You do? He asked.

"Of course I do. You're married to my cousin, which makes you a cousin to me too. So maybe I should be kissing you as well. Especially since this is a grand opening and all."

"No, no thanks. I'll pass."

"Will you, now?" Kimberly said. She began running her hand through Tonya's hair. She noticed a tense look come across Carl's face.

"You mean you don't want to kiss me?" Tonya asked. "I want to kiss you. I think that we should do this all together especially since your friend is not coming. I would love to see you interact with the both of us."

"Me too," Kimberly said again. Now running her hand across Tonya's breast.

"Kimberly, stop it. Maybe you guys need to take this into the bedroom. I don't want, I mean, I don't need to see this. It's personal between the two of you and it's none of my business."

"What's the matter, Carl you can't take the sight of someone else's hands on me?" Kimberly asked as she took Tonya's hand and placed it on her left breast.

Tonya cupped Kimberly's breast and pulled her closer. She put her lips on Kimberly's neck.

"Oh my God, stop it." Carl said. Kimberly noticed that he was becoming upset.

"What's wrong, Carl. Don't get angry. This is what you wanted right? An open marriage?"

"I don't give a damn about this marriage. I already told you that."

"Then tell us what's really wrong, Carl," Tonya said. "I mean, you are a big strong man from the looks of you and I know you can handle watching two women together. This is every man's fantasy, isn't it?"

"Tonya, you know, look, please stop it."

"Stop what? I'm not doing anything," she said between kisses on Kimberly's neck.

Kimberly began to moan in pleasure.

"Tonya, stop kissing her neck," Carl said as he grabbed her hand off of Kimberly's breast.

"Oh my God. What are you doing, Carl?" Kimberly asked.

"She shouldn't be touching you like that," he said.

"Why not? She can do whatever she wants. She's a grown woman."

"Yes, but she's pregnant," he said.

"What?" Kimberly asked.

"You heard me. She's pregnant and it's my baby. Like I said earlier, I can't do this anymore. I just need all of this to stop. Every time I think I've got everything figured out something crazy happens. I've had enough and I need to put all of this to rest. No more games."

"What games are you talking about, Carl? There have been no games," Tonya said.

"Yes, there have been, Tonya. I have not been totally honest with you or Kim and now is the time to lay it all out in the open."

"Well, what have you not been honest about? I know that you have been nothing but good to me. I just wanted to make sure that we could be together by any means necessary. So, when Kim told me that you guys were opening your relationship, I thought that it would be a great opportunity for us to be together. So, I immediately asked her if I could be a part of the grand opening."

"No, Tonya. That's not the truth. I told you that I was going to break up with her today and that I would be coming to you to be yours forever. I didn't tell you that we were doing this grand opening thing, and that Kimberly was under the impression that we were going to stick this marriage out. I had you believing two different things and that was not right. The truth is I just want to be with you. I don't want this marriage anymore and I told Kim that just a few minutes before you got here."

"Wait a minute. Everybody needs to slow down. What the hell is going on here?" Kimberly asked, feigning confusion.

"Kim, Tonya and I are expecting a baby. This isn't the first time that she's been pregnant by me. We were a couple about thirteen years ago, and I betrayed and left her. This was before I met you. I convinced her to get an abortion and then I wasn't there for her when she actually went to get it. I tricked her into going into the room by herself and then I disappeared out of her life. I met you about three years later, but I never stopped thinking about what I had done to her. I have been living with the guilt of that part of my life since. I felt guilty on our wedding day because I knew that I was marrying the wrong woman. When you gave birth to both children, I felt that God was somehow punishing me by giving me two beautiful children; children that I didn't deserve. Then about a year ago, I saw Tonya at a coffee shop and from then on, it's been my quest to make it all up to her. I gave her my heart, along with my sincerest apologies, and I promised that I would never put another person or woman in front her."

"So, you've been seeing her all this time, all the time that I have been sitting here crying over you and our marriage. Here I am feeling bad that our children are going to be from a broken home, and you have been planning and promising her to do just that to them. You are such a sorry excuse for a man."

"That's okay. I'll be a sorry excuse to you but, as long as you don't see me that way, then my world is perfect, Tonya."

"As long as she doesn't see you that way? Wow, that is priceless. Unbelievable."

"Tonya, please baby. Just say something. Tell me what's going on. Tell me that you love me. Tell me that you didn't get rid of the baby today. Tell me that you really aren't here to be with your cousin or to help us commemorate this grand opening nonsense. Tell me that it's just going to be the two of us and we can walk out of here right now. No questions asked."

Tonya looked at Kimberly. Kimberly nodded to her, indicating that it was time that she told him the truth as well.

"Carl, when you left me at that abortion clinic, I didn't know what to do. I didn't know how I was going to make it through what was left of my life. Hell, I didn't think I had a life. God was going to strike me down for what I had done to my baby. And what was strange is I knew that when I went into that room without you that you were already gone and that you wouldn't be there when I returned. It was partially why I went through with it. I did not want to go through the life of having your child and not having you as well. I didn't want to be one of those mothers that spent all of their time at the courthouse trying to get child support. I also didn't want to do that to the child. I knew that the decision I was making was the best at the time, but I still could not live with myself for doing it. I thought about trying to find you, but I figured if you wanted to be found, you would never have left. My cousin Kim and I used to be so tight as young children, but she moved away with her father when we were fifteen. It had been two years since I had seen her when I met you, and I had not seen her since, until a few months ago when I bumped into her at the mall. She told me she was married and had two kids and of course, she showed me pictures. That's when I saw that it was you. I wanted to tell her, but I didn't want to hurt her. I continued to see you because part of me was mad at her as well. Because she got to spend a life with you, and I got to have a life of hurt and shame. Then when you kept apologizing and telling me that you wanted to be with me, I initially thought that it was my chance to have the life that I've always wanted. That lasted for about two minutes because I realized how angry I was at you and realized that I could never ever love you again. You are not capable of love or loyalty, for that matter. I decided I needed to get the courage to tell my cousin the truth about us. I mean she was back into my life, and I never wanted to lose her again. Especially not over some trifling man."

"Tonya, I said I'm sorry."

"Yes, you are sorry. Please let me finish talking. Anyway, I told Kim about you and me from the past, but I omitted our present for a few weeks. I wanted to make sure that you were serious and that you really wanted to be with me. So that's when I told you that I was pregnant. I wanted to see if that would make you run away again. Instead, it made you want to be a family with me. It was then that I realized that you were in it to stay and that your heart was totally invested. That's when I decided to tell Kim the whole truth."

"And that is when I decided to tell you about this open relationship thing?" Kim smiled. "I figured you would just try to introduce Tonya into our relationship, but instead, you didn't. You only wanted to keep her to yourself."

"So, when she told you about the open relationship, you told me, and that's when all of the planning began. Imagine how easy it was for me to know that both of you had ulterior motives and that you were both trying to play one another. But I realized that my cousin had done nothing wrong to me and that it was only you, so I ceased the opportunity to repay you for all that you had done to me."

Kimberly watched as Carl sat down on the couch. He placed his head in his hands.

"So, is there a baby?" He asked.

"I'm getting there. Just be a bit more patient," Tonya said. "Kimberly told me that you were inviting someone over and she didn't know who it was. She asked me to try to find out from you. Of course, when I asked you what your plan was, you spilled the beans instantly. And I know you only did it because you were trying to convince me of your dedication to our relationship. So, you told me that you were going to use the babysitter so you could make Kim angry and make her want to leave you. Then you tried to sell me on the idea that you might only actually have to have sex with Cindy as a part of the plan, which I knew was crap. But I agreed to it and told Kim about your plan."

"Can I tell the rest from here?" Kim asked.

"Sure Cousin, go right ahead."

Carl looked at Kimberly with every ounce of anger that he had in his body.

"Aw, don't look at me like that, Carl. You are going to like this. So, when Tonya told me that you had asked Cindy to be your grand opening partner, I thought that it was very clever of you. That would have been a great reason for me to leave you. But did you really think that I was going to just let her come in here and have sex with you. After all, she and I had been through? Anyway, I called Cindy, and I asked her if you approached her about it yet and you hadn't. Looks like I beat you to her, so I prepared her for you and told her to go along with it when you did. When you finally did ask her, you know she couldn't wait to tell me. She said she was offended that you would be so low as to try pull her into your extramarital affairs. I think you forgot that she used to be a married woman too and her husband cheated on her, then left her for another woman. So, she agreed to your little proposition, and we were all set. Now, all I had to do was try to find a man to show up on my behalf. Unfortunately, and contrary to your personal beliefs, there was no one that I thought was worthy enough to step foot into my home and I realized that I didn't need to be with anyone else. I just had to find a way to emphasize to you that I was no longer your little puppy dog and that I had my own life and that I could go on without you."

"So, one day when we were on the phone," Tonya interrupted. "I told Kim that I was still angry at you and that I wished there was a way for me to get back at you and we came up with the idea of me coming as her grand opening partner. We knew that you would look like you saw a ghost when you saw me. But the one thing we had not planned on was Cindy changing her mind about the whole thing. Apparently, she grew a conscious and chickened out at the last minute. By the way, she called us both before she texted you. This worked out especially in my favor because you were already in panic mode when I skipped out on that little boy that you had watching my house and from the lack of response that you were getting from me to your text messages. When Kim called to confirm that I was still coming, I figured that it was time to put you out of your misery."

"Isn't this all so exciting, Carl?" Kimberly asked. "Don't you feel stupid. Don't you feel like a fool for how we played you."

"No, Kim. I really don't. I don't care what either of you did? I just know that I love this woman and I have loved her my whole life. I can forgive anything that she's done or planned. Tonya, we can start over and put all of this childish stuff behind us. Let's just forget it all. It's okay. I forgive you."

"No, Carl. You don't get it. I don't forgive you. I could never forgive you. I loved you to the end of the earth and back. I would have never done anything like you've done to me. I would have stayed with you through thick and thin. Through the rain or storm. I would never have betrayed you. I trusted you and I believed whatever you said," Tonya said with tears streaming from her eyes. "You have to pay for what you've done to me. I will not be able to let this go until I feel like you've got what you have had coming to you all this time."

"So, here is the clincher," Kimberly jumped in again. "No Carl, she is not pregnant. She never was. It was only a gimmick to ensure that you were head over heels for her, so she could break your heart like she is doing now, and I can watch the whole thing. There was never any baby and she has been playing the whole time."

Kim watched as Carl balled his hands into

fists. He jumped up from the couch and into Tonya's face.

"Is that true? There's no baby. There never was a baby?"

Tonya did not answer him. She only looked up at him as his tall frame towered over her.

"Get out of her face, Carl."

"Don't tell me what to do, Kim."

"She is still my cousin and that means she's family, so you better get out of her face."

"Kim, it's okay. He's not going to do anything to me. I know him. He loves me too much."

Kimberly watched as Tonya stared directly into Carl's face.

"Carl, there was a time when I used to dream of us getting back together and becoming a family. I would go back and forth between that and seeing you unhappy. I felt that I would rejoice in your pain in exchange for my own. But instead, today, I just feel sorry for you. You don't have a clue. You never have. You have never known how to love or to be loved. I know that you lived a hard childhood and that you were always searching for someone to be there for you. I always thought that I would fill that void for you, but I realize at this very moment, that you have to do that for yourself. You have to love yourself before you can love anyone else. I know that you hate yourself and that happiness is not something that you will ever experience. You are not the type of person that knows how to embrace it. You wouldn't know real love if it slapped you in the face but, that's not your fault. It's the result of irresponsible parenting. Your mother never got it right with you and as a result, you are this defective individual that doesn't know how to interact with anyone. You are a pathetic being and you would be crazy to think that I would want to be in the same room with you more less live a life with you. You disgust me and I can't stand it when you stand this close to me. So, like Kim said, you need to back up and get the hell out of my face before we have real problems."

Kim watched as Tonya reached down to the couch and grabbed her purse. She opened it and pulled out a small handgun.

"Tonya, what the hell are you doing?" Kim yelled.

"Kim, he deserves this. I have been waiting for this since he ruined my life."

"Oh, so you're going to shoot me now?" Carl said, leaning even closer to her face. "Do it, Tonya. Don't get scared now. Be a woman, pull the trigger."

"Don't tempt me, Carl. Just back up off me, please."

"Tonya, put the gun down, please,"

Kimberly cried.

"Kim, tell him to get away from me. Every ounce of my being wants to do this."

"Then do it. Haven't you ever heard the saying, don't pull a gun on someone unless you intend to use it?" Carl said. "Do it."

"No Tonya. Don't do it. He's not worth it. Do you want to spend the rest of your life in jail after this? After all that, he's put you through all of these years.

Tonya began to cry harder. She raised the gun and pushed it into Carl's chest.

"You don't have it in you. Just like you didn't have it in you to go to the abortion clinic until I pushed you. You are nothing but a pathetic little girl, which is why I left you there in the first place. I knew that you couldn't handle it then and I know you can't now. Put the gun down so we can all just get the hell out of here and be done with this whole thing."

"Tonya, he's not worth it girl. Let him go. Please give me the gun."

Kimberly moved over to where Tonya was standing. She put her hand on top of the hand that Tonya was using to hold the gun.

"Let me have it," Kimberly said. "Don't give him the satisfaction.

Kimberly stepped behind Tonya and wrapped her other arm around her waist. She still had her hand on top of the gun.

"We are in this together girl. My hand is on the gun too. You shoot, we go down together. You don't and we walk out of here together. I'm here with you. I will never leave you. You or I, we don't need him. He's nothing and he's not good enough for either of us. Don't let him bring you down to his pathetic level."

"I don't have to bring her down, she's already there. She's always been. She's always been so naive."

"Shut up, Carl. I'm trying to save your stupid life. Just shut the hell up."

Kimberly put pressure on Tonya's arm, causing her to lower the gun. She put up no resistance. Kim let out a loud cry in the process. As soon as she lowered it, Carl reached over and slapped Tonya across her face, causing her to fall to the floor.

"Don't you ever pull a gun on me again. You must have lost your damn mind," he yelled.

Kim watched, in what seemed to be slow motion, as Tonya raised the gun, pointed it at Carl's head and pulled the trigger. The bullet entered his left eye and he instantly stopped moving. After what was only a second but seemed like forever, he fell forward on top of Tonya."

"Tonya, no!" Kim yelled.

TARA MONTGOMERY

17 WATCH WHAT YOU ASK FOR

"Oh my God. What have you done? Tonya, what have you done?" Kimberly screamed. She ran over to the where Carl had fallen on top of Tonya. She rolled his body over and off of her.

"Carl, can you hear me? Carl, please don't be dead. Oh my God, oh my God," Kim cried. "Tonya, we need to call 911. Tonya, call the ambulance," Kim said as he pulled Carl's head up on her lap. She looked down at him and watched as his head fell to the side.

"Come on, Carl, please don't be dead.

Kimberly looked over at Tonya, who did not move. She only stared at Carl's face. She did not speak or look like she was even breathing. She just sat in a catatonic trance.

"Tonya," Kimberly yelled. "Snap out of it and call the ambulance. Carl, hold on baby. Don't die."

She turned his head back toward her lap and

looked at the hole that used to be his eye. She could feel the warm blood run down her knee from the back of his head.

"Oh, Carl no, no, no. Please don't do this. Tonya," she yelled. "Tonya."

Still there was no movement from her. Kim placed Carl's head on the carpet and ran to the bar where she had left her cell phone. She dialed the emergency services and waited.

"911," said the operator. "What's your emergency?"

"A man has been shot," Kimberly yelled into the phone. "My husband has been shot. Please help him. He's dying."

"Ma'am, please slow down. I can't understand you. I need you to calm down and tell me what's going on."

Kimberly took a deep breath and began speaking again.

"My husband has been shot," she said into the phone.

"Okay, Ma'am. Is he still alive?" The operator asked.

"I don't think so. He doesn't look like he's breathing."

"Where is he now, Ma'am?"

"He's lying on the floor."

"What about you? Are you any danger? Is the person that shot him still in the area?"

"Yes, she's still here but I'm not in any

danger."

"Are you sure, Ma'am? Because if she's still there, I need you to get to a safe place until we can get the police over there."

"I'm not in any danger. I'm sure."

"Where are you located, Ma'am?" The operator asked.

"I'm at my house. It's at 2902 Raycrest Drive."

"Okay, Ma'am I'm sending someone. They'll will be there shortly. Just sit tight."

"Okay, thank you. Please hurry," Kimberly said and ended the call.

She walked back over to Tonya, who was still sitting on the floor. The gun was still in her hand, but both hands were rested on the floor.

"Tonya, are you okay? Tonya, talk to me."

Kimberly put her arm around Tonya's shoulder and began rubbing her head.

"Tonya, it's okay. Just give me the gun."

Kimberly put her hand on the gun and removed it from Tonya's hand without any struggle. She stood up and placed the gun on the bar. She walked back over to Tonya and tried to help her up.

"Come on, let me get you off of this floor. Sit up here on the couch. At that moment, Tonya began speaking.

"I didn't mean to shoot him. He was just saying so much, and I was getting tense. Then he slapped me, and I was just going to hit him with the gun, but my finger was on the trigger and the next thing I know, it went off. I didn't mean to shoot him, Kim. I'm so sorry," she cried. "He's dead isn't he. Oh my God, I killed him. I didn't mean to kill him. I'm a murderer. I can't go to jail. I didn't mean shoot him, Kim."

"Tonya, calm down. It's all right. The police are on their way. We will just explain to them what happened when they get here. They will want to hear our side of the story anyway."

"No, they are going to want to take us to jail. They are going to look at me like some jealous woman who killed her lover. I didn't mean to kill him. I just wanted to scare him. I wanted him to know what it felt like to be scared like I was."

"I know you didn't mean it, Tonya," Kim said, trying to keep her calm until the police arrived. She knew that Tonya was unstable and that she should not do anything to make this situation any worse. She did not want Tonya to cause any more problems before the police got there."

"Kim, you know that I didn't mean to kill him, right? You know that I would never do anything like that right?" Tonya pleaded.

"Yes, I know."

"Kim, please call my mother and tell her that I'm sorry. Tell her that I didn't mean to hurt anyone."

"I will. I'll call her right after the police get here."

"I can't go to jail, Kim. I won't survive. Plus, I'm pregnant."

"What do you mean you're pregnant? I thought you said there was no baby?"

"There wasn't one before, but I took a pregnancy test this morning and I really am pregnant. It's Carl's baby. I know I should have told you and I'm sorry. I couldn't tell you that I was still sleeping with him after we had both decided that we were done with him. I loved him so much that I couldn't resist him. When I found out this morning, I got angry all over again and it was my intention to get rid of the baby. I was just going to wait until my next payday to take care of it. I wasn't going to ever tell him about it. Now I won't be able to do it. I'll go to jail, and they are going to make me have the baby. I can't have a baby in jail. I can't go to jail," Tonya cried.

Kimberly noticed that she was getting excited again. Kimberly reached to touch her.

"It's all right. We will figure this out. I promise."

"Don't touch me," Tonya said, pulling away. "This is all your fault, you and Carl. It was your bright idea to do this grand opening mess. If the two of you hadn't concocted this dumb idea, I would never have come over here and he wouldn't be dead."

As much as Kimberly wanted to tell her to shut the hell up and take responsibility for her actions, she didn't say a word. She wanted to tell Tonya, that had she been woman enough to do that all those years ago, maybe things would be different today. She was the one that chose to have an abortion. She walked her own two legs to the abortion clinic. She let him convince her to make the decision. She got pregnant by him, and she was the one that fell in love with him. All of that was Tonya's own responsibility. No one made her do any of those things. Each person is responsible for the decisions that they make, and they must learn to live with those decisions. It was also Tonya's decision to bring a gun here today. She made the decision to pull it from her purse and to point it at Carl. All of this was of her freewill. No one made any of those decisions for her.

"Okay, fine. I won't touch you. I was just trying to help you. Make sure that you are okay."

"I don't need you to take care of me. I can take care of myself."

"I know you can. I was just showing that I'm here for you. Remember, we're cousins and I love you," Kimberly said.

"You don't love me. You only wanted to use

me to get back at your husband. You had been putting up with him for all these years and you were fed up. You are just as pathetic as I am. He brainwashed you too. He made you believe that you were going to be together forever and that he was the loving husband. Only, you didn't know that he had secrets, dirty secrets. I bet you don't know anything about his past. If you did, you would have known about me years ago. Did you know that his father killed himself in front of Carl when he was fourteen years old? I bet you didn't. Did you know that he blamed himself for it because his mother told him that it was his fault? Carl's mother told his father that Carl was somebody else's son and that she was leaving him, so he shot himself right in front of the wife and kid. Carl was tearing up ever since and he blamed himself for the whole thing. You don't know anything. You are just as lost as I am. Maybe it should be you and I lying on the floor. Not Carl. He's been through enough already."

"Tonya, you are just nervous. It's going to be okay," Kim said, realizing that this situation was starting to go out of control.

"Stop telling me it's going to be okay. It's not okay." Tonya ran over to the bar and picked the gun up again. She pointed it at Kimberly.

"Tonya, you're right. This is not okay. And it's only going to get worse. You need to put the gun down. This is not going to make it any better. What would shooting me prove?"

"It won't prove anything, but it will make you pay for bringing us all here together. Somebody has got to pay for this horrible situation and it's not going to be me," Tonya said, crying again.

"Nobody has to pay. This was a mistake. I know you didn't mean to shoot him," Kimberly said, raising her hands overhead to show Tonya that she was in surrender mode.

"I might be the one that shot Carl, but you are the one that killed him. You killed him when you stood at the alter and said I do with him. He died inside that very day. You heard him say that today. And you made it worse when you had those two bastards for him. Now, they don't have a daddy and it's all your fault. You should be the one lying down there. Not my sweet Carl."

Kimberly began to wonder where the police were and why they had not arrived yet. She had always known them to come quickly whenever there was a shooting and now, they were taking forever. She thought that they might be outside and were trying to get into the house. She wished that she had told the operator to tell them all to come to the basement.

"Tonya, you don't mean all of that. Carl was a mean man. He did a lot of bad things to a lot of people. Anything that's happened to him is his own fault."

"No, it's not his fault. Nothing he did meant that he wanted to die. He was only trying to fix things. He wanted to work them out with me, and you were just too jealous to let that happen. So, you did whatever it took to stop us from being happy. You talked me into all of this and now look where it's got you. Look where it got us."

"Tonya, I don't know what else to say. Please put the gun down. You don't want to shoot me."

"Don't tell me what I don't want to do, Kim. I want you to say that this is all your fault. You are going to tell the police that you did this because you were just too jealous to let him go."

"I'll do whatever you say, I just need you to put the gun down."

"Freeze, police," Kimberly heard a male voice say from the top of the stairs. From where she stood near the bar, she could not see him. She assumed that he had a gun pointed at Tonya who was standing in the direct line of vision from the top of the stairs.

"Tonya, please do what they say. Don't make this situation any worse."

"You stop talking to me," Tonya yelled.

"Put the gun down," the male voice yelled

again.

"Officer, it wasn't me. It was her," Tonya yelled up the stairs.

"Just put the gun down and we can talk about it," he said.

"I didn't mean to shoot him."

"That's fine, Ma'am but I need you to put the gun down."

"I can't put it down. Not right now."

Kimberly saw the officer's foot touch the bottom stair. She stood where she was with her hands still above her head.

"Ma'am, are you okay?" The officer asked as he slid around Tonya and over to Carl's body. He squatted down and checked Carl's pulse.

"Yes sir," I'm fine," Kimberly responded.

"Of course she's okay. She caused all of this, so now she's snug as a bug in a rug," Tonya said.

The police officer stood up with his gun still trained on Tonya.

"Ma'am, I need you to put your weapon down."

"I'm so sorry but she needs to pay for making me kill the best thing that's ever happened to me. She needs to pay."

Kimberly closed her eyes and dived to the floor. She knew that Tonya was about to pull the trigger. As she hit the floor, she heard a shot ring out. She wrapped her arms around her head and waited for it all to go black. After a few seconds of silence, she lifted her head.

"It's okay, Ma'am. It's over," the officer said.

Kimberly looked around and noticed that Tonya was laying on the floor.

"Oh my God, you killed her."

"No, she's not dead. It's only a shoulder wound. Hey Tyrone, get those EMS guys down here," he said into a small radio that was attached to his right shoulder."

"Roger," said the voice over the radio.

After a few seconds, Kimberly heard a lot of footsteps coming down the stairs. She stood up from the floor and sat down on the couch. The room was flooded with more officers and a few EMS guys.

"Ma'am, can you tell me what happened here?" said the officer that had just saved her life.

Kimberly began to cry hysterically. She could not believe that things had turned out the way they did. She only wanted to show Carl that she was a strong woman and that she was going to be going on the rest of her life without him. She did not think that he would end up dead. She was going to make it so they all could live happier lives, and no one was going to be subject to either of the other's unhappiness again. She just wanted to let the world know that she had changed and that she was in control. She took it as a bonus that her favorite cousin was back in her life.

"Ma'am let's go upstairs and away from here. It might make things a bit easier for you."

Kimberly let him help her off the couch. She looked at Carl, who lay on the floor in a puddle of blood that had spilled from the back of his head. She could not believe that he was actually dead. As angry as she had been at him and as much as he had hurt her over the years, she never would have wished this fate upon him.

"Oh my God," she said as they walked away and up the stairs. She knew she wanted to live the rest of her life without him, but she had not intended for her children to do the same.

"What will I tell my children," she cried. "Oh my God, what about my children."

PART FIVE

18 THE FINALE

The brightness of the sun shining through the window awakened Kimberly. She looked through squinted eyes at the clock across the room. It had only been one hour since she fell asleep. It had been a long night and she had to stay at her parent's house because her home and been identified as a crime scene. Kimberly closed her eyes and wished that it had all been a dream. She knew that it wasn't because she would have awakened in her own bed with Carl beside her. Instead, she was back in her old bedroom. She was a bit relieved that her parents were away on vacation because then she would have to explain all of this to them. She was still trying to understand it herself.

The police kept her in the small interrogation room for most of the night asking her many of the same questions. Kimberly kept giving them the same answers. Nothing had changed. She assumed that they believed that she would remember something different or that maybe she would change her story. There was no story to change. It had happened just the way she had told them and as much as she wished that it could be different, it was the same thing each time. Kimberly had taken some of the blame for her part in it all. Tonya was right when she said that if she had not made the plan to bring them all together, then none of this would have happened. She was only thinking of herself. She wanted to see Carl hurt and embarrassed, but most of all, she wanted to feel liberated again. Cindy had warned her to handle things differently. She had advised her to just tell Carl how she felt and to just walk away from the marriage without all the games. There was a part of Kimberly that wanted to listen to Cindy, and she was even considering it during their conversation. It was the next talk that she had with Tonya that changed her mind. Tonya seemed content with her idea, which made it easy for Kimberly to be comfortable. She had no idea that Tonya intended to kill Carl. She would have never thought in a thousand years that her cousin would have come to her house with a gun in her purse. Kimberly realized at this moment that she really did not know Tonya anymore. They were sisters when they were young girls, but Kimberly did not know the grown woman that she had become. She never thought to sit down and catch up with her cousin and when she learned that Carl had been in a relationship with her, there was a part of Kimberly that felt like she had won the prize. This woman was here crying over something from so many years ago. To Kimberly, Tonya should have long gotten over it, but since she had not, it was an opportunity to catch Carl in yet another of his adulterous affairs. It was supposed to be short, sweet, and to the point, with everyone living happily ever after. If they all couldn't be happy, they were at least supposed to be alive. No one was supposed to be dead.

When the interrogation at the police station was complete, Kimberly asked if she could go to the hospital to see Tonya. The police denied her request and said that Tonya was a murder suspect and was not allowed to have visitors. They reassured Kimberly when Tonya came out of surgery and told her that she would be just fine. They would interrogate her as soon as she was strong enough to answer questions.

Kimberly opened her eyes and stared at the ceiling. She knew that she was going to have to tell the children that their daddy was gone, but she did not know how she was going to do that. She did not know if they would understand that he was never coming back. She didn't know if she should tell them how he died. How will they ever know how much Carl cared for them and how much he loved them? They would never know that he would walk to the end of the earth and back for them. Part of the reason that he died was because he felt so guilty about how great they were and how he didn't believe that he was good enough to be called their father. Kimberly began to cry as she thought about it.

She thought of calling Cindy, but she decided that she would take a shower first. It was still early, and she knew that they would all still be asleep. She didn't want to wake them. She knew that Cindy hadn't heard the news yet or else she would have called Kimberly by now. She climbed from the bed and walked into the adjourning bathroom. She turned the shower on and picked up the toothbrush that her mother kept in the bathroom for her. Her mother kept her bedroom ready because she said she never knew when she might need it. Not to mention, it was the room that the kids stayed in when they came to visit.

Kimberly brushed her teeth, removed the clothes that she had been wearing from the day before. She had slept in them, and they were still stained with Carl's blood. She stepped into the shower. Kimberly let the water run over her head and down her body. The hot water felt good on her skin and helped her to relax a bit. She took a deep breath and as she exhaled, tears began to pour from her eyes. She cried for Carl.

She cried for Tonya. She cried for her kids and most of all, she cried for herself. She did not know what kind of person she had become. She didn't want to be this woman that caused people to die in the midst of her vindication. She only wanted happiness and joy in her life. At this moment, she didn't know if she would ever experience any of those things again.

After her long fit of crying and letting the water wash away her tears, she lathered up a few times, rinsed and finished her shower. She looked into the closet, where her mother told her to leave a few pieces of clothing for safekeeping. I guess this was one of those just-in-case situations. She pulled out a pair of jeans and a t-shirt. She put them on and then lay back on the bed. She reached for her cell phone and found her mother's name in her contacts. When she located it, she thought of hitting the call button but then stopped. It was too earlier to call her as well, but she needed someone that she could talk to. A feeling of fear had come over her, and there was no one that she could call. She just wanted to be able to cry on someone's shoulder. Carl used to be her go-to in situations such as these, but now he was the situation. Kimberly knew that she was going to have to endure this on her own for a little while longer. She put the phone down and closed her eyes.

When she opened them, she was back in her basement and Carl was standing next to her.

"You were sleeping," he said.

"I was? How long was I out?"

"About fifteen minutes."

"Must have been some kind of dream because you were moaning like crazy."

"Yeah, it was pretty sad," Kimberly, said smiling to herself that it was all a dream. Carl was standing here beside her and none of the shooting or dying had happened.

"Carl, can we call this thing off?" She asked. "I don't want to do it anymore."

"Why? This is all we've been talking about for weeks."

"Yeah, I know but I just have a bad feeling," she said.

"Well, if you don't want to do it, then I don't want to do it," he said.

"Thank you so much."

"So, what do we do now?" He asked.

"We call our people and tell them not to come. Let them know that there will be no grand opening. We are going to keep our marriage closed and it is nobody's business what happens from here on out."

"Okay, let's do it."

"I just think we need to work on us. Let's put all that crazy stuff in the past and move on. From now on, I know nothing and no one but you. You are all that's important in this life and I will never be distracted again," Kimberly confessed.

"All right, I can do the same thing, but I believe it's going to be a lot more work than just talking about it. There are people that I have promised who I'll now have to cut loose,'" Carl said.

"I can live with that, and I can be patient while you take care of it. Now, what about my cousin? What about Tonya?"

"Tonya is one of those that have to be cut off, but in order for this to work, you are going to have to cut her off too."

"I know and I can do that. She's been out of my life all of these years; it won't be hard for me to let her go. I'll do anything to keep you," Kimberly said.

"Will you love me through all of it; through thick and thin, in sickness and in health, until death do us part?"

Yes, yes, and yes," Kimberly said as she watched as blood began to pour from Carl's left eye and down his shirt.

"Carl no," she said as she ran to cover his eyes. "No, Carl, don't do this. Not again. Someone help me."

Kimberly looked behind her to find someone to help her. There was no one else there. She looked back at Carl, but he was gone.

She was in the small interrogation room at the police station and the lights were flashing.

"No, I didn't do it," she said.

A female police officer across the room screamed back at her.

"If you didn't do this, then who did? You know this is all your fault, just confess to it and set yourself free."

"No, I didn't do it. This is not my fault. I didn't have the gun and I wasn't the one that pulled the trigger."

"No, you didn't but you did set up the events for a perfect storm. You set all of the players in place, and you created the perfect conditions. The devil could not have done it better himself. Maybe you are working for him. Maybe he helped you plan the whole thing."

"No, I didn't plan anything but a sexual rendezvous. We were supposed to have sex, not commit murder."

"You are a liar. Please tell the truth so we can all go home."

"Yes, Kim, tell the truth so we can all get out of here," Tonya suddenly appeared at the table that was in the middle of the room."

"No, Tonya. You tell them that you did this and that I had nothing to do with it. Tell them how I did not know that you had a gun in your purse. Tell them that you did all of this on your own. This is not what we planned. We just planned to make him squirm a little bit. It wasn't supposed to get this far out of hand."

"Oh, come on Kim. You knew that I was unstable. You could tell every time you talked to me, but you didn't want to admit it to yourself because you only want to acknowledge the things that get you what you want. You are so selfish that you had an opportunity to save your husband's life, but your greed would not let you do it. Now, it's all over and it's too late. You are going to jail and there's nothing you can do about it," Tonya laughed.

"I'm not going to jail. You are. You did this. I'm not taking the wrap for you. I never wanted to be part of any murder. I didn't discuss it with you. You're just crazy."

"I might be crazy, but you are the one fighting with your own mind to prove innocence to yourself."

Kimberly sat up on the bed. She looked around. She was still in her bedroom in her mother's house. It was all still real. Carl was gone and she was alone. There was no one left for her to talk to at the moment. She looked at the clock and though her sleep had been restless, she realized that she had slept for two hours. She picked up her cell phone and dialed Cindy's phone number. There was no answer and after the fourth ring, Cindy's voicemail activated. Kimberly waited for the greeting message and then began to speak.

"Cindy, I don't know if you saw the news yet, but I was wondering if you could let the kids stay there with you until I come and get them. Please call me as soon as possible, whether you saw the news or not." She ended the call and put the phone down on the bed.

Kimberly had not seen the news, but she assumed that their story was all over the local news channels. She was not going to leave her parent's home. She did not want to find out the hard way that the whole city knew that her husband was dead. Also, the whole neighborhood would see the crime scene tape that was strung up around her entire yard. She did not want to field any questions from anyone else about what had happened. She knew that there would be a time and a place to answer all these questions but, right now was not the time.

Kimberly got up from the bed and walked to the other side of the house to the kitchen. She pulled a glass from the cabinet and poured herself a glass of water from the jug that her mother kept inside the refrigerator. She sat down at the kitchen table as instant memories began to flood her mind. She and her parents had shared numerous Saturdays at this table doing crossword puzzles and playing board games. They would compete to see who could finish the Sunday paper puzzle first. It was the hardest of the puzzles that were put in the paper every day of the week. A smile crossed her face as she thought about it. She finished her water and returned to the room.

Kimberly sat back down on the bed, and she continued to think of her parents. They always let her know how proud they were of her. She had a great childhood because of it. She was never afraid to try anything, which is why it was hard to understand why she let Carl mess with her self-esteem for so many years. She had just loved him so much and had put so much into their relationship that somewhere along the way, she had lost herself in him. When this happened, she was lost when he was not there with her or when he decided that he no longer wanted to be married to her.

She picked up her phone and found her mother's name again. This time she would press send and she would tell her mother all that was going on. She knew that once she heard her mother's voice, the floodgates would open. Kimberly knew that she would cry like she did when she was a little girl. She knew that she would not be able to contain herself and that she wouldn't have to because her mother would encourage her to express feelings even if she didn't agree with them. She was told to always tell the people around her how she felt and to never be ashamed of what her feelings were.

Once her mother realized what was happening, she would put her father on the phone. He would then say that they were on their way home and get on the next thing, smoking from wherever they were. Yes, Kimberly knew that her parents would be a mainstay in her corner and that they would not let her blame herself for any of it. Not only would they make her accept the situation for what it was, but they would find a way to help her deal with it and they would be beside her though every second of it. Kimberly knew that she had the most understanding parents on the planet and that there was nothing that she could do to make them abandon her.

She hit call and waited for the phone to ring. As she waited, she began to feel better already. She could fear her breathing begin to calm. She anticipated hearing her mother say that everything was going to be okay and that they would go through it all together. Her mother would make sure the children were taken care of, as they all would be living in the same house. Kimberly closed her eyes and waited for the sound of her mother's voice.

"Hello," the beautiful voice said. Tears began to stream from her eyes. "Kimberly, what's wrong? Is everything okay?

"Mommy, it's all messed up and I don't know what to do?" She cried.

"What's messed up, Kimberly? What's going on?" Her mother asked. "Kinston, something is wrong with your daughter."

"Mom, it's Carl. He's dead."

"What do you mean he's dead? Kimberly, what are you saying?"

"Give me the phone," she heard her father say. "Kim, this is your father. What the hell is going on? Where are you?"

"I'm at your house and Carl is dead."

"What? What happened? No, don't tell me. Your mother and I are on our way."

"Thank you, Daddy. Thank you."

ABOUT THE AUTHOR

Tara Montgomery is a retired United States Army solider with 25 years of service. She resides in San Antonio, Texas. She is the author of three novels, Melody's Clear, Sister Soldier, and Two Hours Til Open. Tara holds a B.S. in Criminal Justice from the University of Maryland University College and a Master of Social Work from the University of Southern California. She discovered her love of writing in elementary school when she won a statewide essay writing contest. Her current research is in the history and theoretical causality of African American homosexuality during slavery and its effects on today's African American community. Tara is available for book signings and speaking engagements. To learn more visit www.taramontgomery.net or contact her at tarat.montgomery@gmail.com.